Delicious Prey

Debbie Hope

Copyright © 2024 by Debbie Hope

All rights reserved.

No part of this publication may be reproduced, distributed, or transmitted in any form or by any means, including photocopying, recording, or other electronic or mechanical methods, without the prior written permission of the publisher, except as permitted by U.S. copyright law. For permission requests, contact [include publisher/author contact info].

The story, all names, characters, and incidents portrayed in this production are fictitious. No identification with actual persons (living or deceased), places, buildings, and products is intended or should be inferred.

Book Cover designer: Crimson Phoenix Creations

NO AI TRAINING: Without in any way limiting the author's [and publisher's] exclusive rights under copyright, any use of this publication to "train" generative artificial intelligence (AI) technologies to generate text is expressly prohibited. The author reserves all rights to license uses of this work for generative AI training and development of machine learning language models.

Content Warning

For those who may be sensitive to certain mental and emotional stimulus, be aware that this book contains cursing, threats, murder, domestic abuse, stalking, and sexual scenes with anal play, hunting, Dom/sub dynamic.

There my be other emotional stimuli not mentioned here that was missed, so if at any time you feel uncomfortable and unable to continue reading, please consider closing the book and walking away for your own health. You matter, too.

If you're willing to continue reading despite this warning, I hope you enjoy the book and all it has to offer.

Contents

CHAPTER ONE	1
CHAPTER TWO	8
CHAPTER THREE	14
CHAPTER FOUR	19
CHAPTER FIVE	24
CHAPTER SIX	29
CHAPTER SEVEN	35
CHAPTER EIGHT	41
CHAPTER NINE	47
CHAPTER TEN	54
CHAPTER ELEVEN	58
CHAPTER TWELVE	65
CHAPTER THIRTEEN	70

CHAPTER FOURTEEN	75
CHAPTER FIFTEEN	79
CHAPTER SIXTEEN	83
CHAPTER SEVENTEEN	88
CHAPTER EIGHTEEN	93
CHAPTER NINETEEN	98
CHAPTER TWENTY	106
CHAPTER TWENTY-ONE	111
CHAPTER TWENTY-TWO	116
CHAPTER TWENTY-THREE	123
CHAPTER TWENTY-FOUR	129
CHAPTER TWENTY-FIVE	135
CHAPTER TWENTY-SIX	142
CHAPTER TWENTY-SEVEN	149
CHAPTER TWENTY-EIGHT	155
CHAPTER TWENTY-NINE	159
CHAPTER THIRTY	165
CHAPTER THIRTY-ONE	171
CHAPTER THIRTY-TWO	176
CHAPTER THIRTY-THREE	181
CHAPTER THIRTY-FOUR	186
CHAPTER THIRTY-FIVE	192
CHAPTER THIRTY-SIX	199

CHAPTER THIRTY-SEVEN	205
CHAPTER THIRTY-EIGHT	211
CHAPTER THIRTY-NINE	216
CHAPTER FORTY	223
About the author	231
Also by	232

CHAPTER ONE

Savannah

Layers of foundation will cover the bruises on my skin, but they won't help cover the bruises on my soul.

My husband comes out of his office; a scowl on his angry face making me shiver. His hands in hard fists, the thin line of his lips makes my heart flutter like a dying bird struggling to survive the ravening jaws of a rabid beast. He acts like that sometimes. A beast wrecking destruction and ruin to anything in its devouring sight. His malevolent stare batters at me, telling me time will be my enemy. The malevolence, a living, breathing being, stalking and prowling through the room with us. Searching for its prey, which is me. Hovering, for its time to strike. Why he hates me so after eighteen years of marriage, I have no idea.

I don't want any more beatings, but I also won't give in to his demands. Maybe that's why he hates me so. No matter how much or often he abuses me, he won't have me. He'll have to tie me up and knock me out first. I won't let him share me with his friends like I'm some kind of toy to be given away as a prize. That's what he wants to do. Share me as some kind of gift to any of them doing him favors.

"Did you call Shaun Hennessy like I told you to?" He throws the words at me as if they're knives to rip through me.

"Yes, and left a message with his secretary to get him to call you back. She wouldn't let me talk with him." My voice trembles and I pretend to be busy working, shuffling through files and papers, trying to hide the way my hands shake. He leans over the desk, grabbing my chin tight in the grasp of two fingers.

"Don't lie to me. She said you never called."

I wince away from his hand, sure there will be a bruise there in a few hours.

"Answer me!" he shouts.

"You didn't ask me a question." I know I'm going to get in trouble for smarting off at him.

"Fucking cunt," he growls, his hand lowering and grabbing my throat, my pulse throbs in his hand as he tightens his grip.

Maybe he'll kill me this time, and I'll be out of my misery. He squeezes my throat tighter and tighter, little by little, stretching my possible death out as long as he can.

"Dave, what's going on here?" Dave's best friend, Conor, says in a slow, disbelieving voice.

Dave drops his hand, and I turn my head. Conor's usually smiling face is set in his don't lie to me cop scowl.

"Nothing, Conor, other than husband and wife stuff." Dave lays his hand on the back of my neck, pinching the skin, telling me to behave. "You probably wouldn't remember what that's like." Conor acts like he never heard the spiteful remark.

I blink back tears at the sharp bite of pain, as if I would tell anyone anyway. He's such a pillar of the community to anyone other than me. A fake, stiff smile spreads across my lips to support the lie.

"So, why are you here, buddy?" Dave asks his best friend.

Conor is one of the ones Dave wants to *lend* me to. I'm an object to my wonderful husband. Why I agreed to marry him, I don't know, other than I fell for his shit lies of love and forever. And the fact my parents pushed me to marry him.

"Thought I'd take you both out to lunch. That new restaurant that opened down the street. I have a reservation. I'm off work for the day." Conor tosses a thoughtful gaze at Dave, I can't tell what he's thinking, if he believes Dave or not. His gaze settles with a slight frown between the two of us and switches quickly back to a smile.

Conor is beautiful in a dangerous, knife-like way. His face is all sharp edges, even at fifty. Way over a foot taller than me and a good five inches on Dave's six feet.

Dave glares at me. "I can't go. There was a miscommunication with a client, and I have to take care of it." When he says miscommunication, I can almost hear the grinding of his teeth, fury pulsing off him in waves. "You two go. Enjoy yourselves, I know Savannah deserves some time off. I've been working her too hard."

I almost choke on my saliva at how nice he's pretending to be. Didn't know he was such a good actor, the red tinge on his face is the only thing revealing how fake he is.

"Well, Savannah, looks like it's just us." Conor claps his hands together, holding one out to lead me out the office. The hand he holds out to me has tattoos on the back, and the t-shirt he wears shows black tattoos swirling up his arm.

I'm not sure what kind of trick Dave is playing and if Conor is in on it. Are they combining forces to see if I'll do it? Let Conor fuck me over my marriage vows? I won't do it. I know things are bad between us, or rather, with him. He either has someone on the side or he is working late nights like he says he is. I vote for the side piece. He doesn't initiate sex as often anymore. Maybe once a week or so. I haven't had sex with him in I don't know how long. I'm thankful he's tired of me. I have to pretend I'm enjoying it when we do or I get punished, and not in a sexy or fun way. Violent, depraved punishments he makes sure I don't enjoy.

I gaze down at the computer, hoping neither one will notice the cold shivers running over my body like I'm in an ice storm. Tears I hope don't turn into icicles fill my eyes, rimming the edges, but don't fall. I continue working as they talk over me; feeling someone's gaze on me. God, I hope it's not Dave. I don't know what I would have done wrong this time.

My fingers type at the computer, doing invoices, a task I don't have to put much thought into, since I have no idea what I'm writing.

"So, Conor, what about Stan Fritch? I heard he committed suicide?"

I can't believe he killed himself. Dave is a criminal defense attorney and got him off for allegedly raping his niece. There was no proof, and the child recanted her accusations. When I saw her on TV, the fear in her eyes was soul destroying. Stan and his brother are close. Deviants. The girl was only five years old when her mother died and only had her father and uncle. Deep down, I knew Stan had done it, maybe her father, too, but the girl wouldn't talk anymore.

"Yeah, I heard about that this morning when I went it. Weird, he killed himself after getting off free."

I lift my gaze, Conor is staring right at me as he talks to Dave, his black as sin eyes telling me things I don't understand. It clutches at my stomach for some reason, with a yearning I've never experienced before. Desires I've never felt before. Passions I've only heard or read about.

My pussy throbs with him steadily gazing at me, in time with my pulse pounding in my ears. I don't know what they're saying. All I can hear is the *thud, thud, thud* of my heart. I don't understand this, I've known Conor since I met Dave. I've never had this burning inside me, this yearning. I snap my gaze away from him as if being thrown from a cliff, my body hurling faster and faster, a jet diving out of control toward its death.

I gaze back at my work, my fingers stumbling over the keys, typing a jumble of catapulted words that have no meaning to my stunted brain. Turning to a drawer, I pull it open, pretending to look for something. Anything. Waiting for them to get out of my space.

"So, Savannah, are you ready to go?"

My head jerks up, his voice echoing, bouncing around like a ball in my head, gazing back at Conor, not believing what he said. I turn my head, slow, expecting to see Dave laughing that he'd let me out of his sight.

Instead, all he says with a bored sigh and wave of his hand is, "Go. Go. I have things to do and don't want to have to listen to your whiny voice."

He's such a bastard, always putting me down in front of people. His friends and clients. You'd think he'd go out of his way to make me look better in their eyes. I know I'm nothing special to look at, plain brown hair, pale blue eyes. Nothing special. Still.

Conor slides a strange glance at Dave out of the corner of his eyes. It's a calculating, scheming, decisive look, like he's now decided on a course of action.

"You're free now." Conor holds a large hand out to me. "Let's go, mouse."

"What?" I squeak, just like a mouse, and the two men laugh. Dave not nicely. Demeaning. Heat rises fast like a tsunami of fire heating my face and ears, burning through my veins in a firestorm of embarrassment.

I start shuffling all my files into a drawer in my desk so it can be locked. "No, don't bother," Dave says. "I might need something later. It'll be good to get away from your annoying squeaking for a while. Go straight home afterwards."

My gaze flies up to Dave, and he's scowling at me already. My heart starts to scurry away like the little mouse Conor accused me of being.

I have no choice. After eighteen years of mental and physical abuse, this is what I have become.

A mouse.

A mouse who might die at any moment, always afraid that each night might be her last. Stomped into oblivion by the one who should be her protector, not her murderer.

CHAPTER TWO

Conor

What is it with this little mouse? Why does she intrigue me so?

Lava burns through my veins at the thought of Dave abusing her. There were signs, but I never knew for sure. She must be good at covering the bruises or they are where no one sees. But it's going to end soon; he'll never get another pervert or killer off again. Unfortunately, I'll have to take it slow, seeing as he's a famous criminal defense attorney, known for his high-profile cases, like the Fritch case.

That was my most difficult. Holding my gun on him, stuffing a gag in his mouth, dragging him to the bathtub, slicing his wrists and filling the tub with warm water. All with gloves on and taking the gag with me. I stood and watched as the life slowly drained out of him, satisfaction ballooning inside me as his eyes turned blank with his death, the water turning a deep red as it filled with his life.

I made sure there was no evidence of my being there and no reason for the detectives who got the case to consider it was anything but exactly a suicide. It would look as if even though Fritch got off, the guilt of what he did to his niece, and I'm sure other girls, ate at him enough to end it all.

Now I needed to find a way to end the reign of Dave Collier getting all these deviants off and abusing his wife. To make it look like an accident.

How this sweet and pure being can be with such a bully, a man more in touch with his position and affluent appearance. When he first started toying with her, I tried to convince her to not give in to his devious smiles and words of love. I knew they were false. Dave and I had been friends since we were twelve. Well, not friends exactly. After I saved him from that beat down, which I found out later he deserved, I kept him in my sights. I pretended to be his best friend because I knew he was trouble. Born thinking he could do no wrong, not understanding right from wrong.

I'd always wanted to be a cop and save people. My father was one, my grandfather and his father. It was expected of me and something I always embraced. Then fifteen years into being a street cop, and then a detective, something changed for me. A big-time serial rapist got off on a legal technicality.

The outrage was nationwide, but there was nothing the courts could do. Dave, the lawyer for Alan Wade, got the rapist off on each count. The girls couldn't name him specifically as their rapist because they didn't see him.

I'll never forget the smirks of triumph both Dave and Alan had on their victorious faces. That was the moment I decided to take matters into my own hands. Change the course of the wrongs the judicial system can create. Rewrite the corruption of the system, make those fuckers face their fate and end them so they can't hurt another person.

"Come on, mouse. Your jailer has set you free for at least a couple hours."

I reach down, grabbing her hand, and pull her out of her chair. She reaches down by her feet under the desk and grabs her purse. Dave watches, his thin lips downturned and silent as he stares at her like a hawk ready to tear open the mouse in its claws and devour its insides.

Savannah turns her head for one last glimpse at her husband, and I pull her out of his sight. She's free. At least for a little while.

I lead her to my Range Rover, opening the door for her and helping her inside. She adjusts herself, setting her bag on the floor by her feet, her fingers roll her wedding ring back and forth nervously. Her eyes stay on her fingers, except for when she shoots quick glances at Dave's office.

He stands at the wide-open door, wrapping his hands on the upper door frame, muscles tight, watching us, a cruel, possessive ownership distorts his lips into an unnatural arch. Dave's a narcissist who thinks he's a man every woman is after, and even though he told her to go with me, he'll punish her in some way.

Terror curls her body as if she can protect herself that way, her face crumples, her green eyes wide.

I slam her door closed so he can't see her through the darkened side windows. Walking around the front of the SUV, I sneak a side glance, and he's still in the same position, his eyes narrowed, watching. He's pissed his toy is being snatched away, even if it's only for a couple hours.

Opening my door, I slide in as if I have no interest in her internal and external conflicts.

"Come on, let's go. Ready for good food?" I add a lot of enthusiasm to my voice, trying to draw her out of her fear.

I push the button to start the car and put it in gear, taking off down Main Street in Bay City. I do love this town where I grew up, but with all the wealthy, corrupt men in this town and into Los Angeles, it's hard to keep this city safe.

We don't talk, I let her wind down from the overabundance of negative emotions from her husband. I need to find a way to get rid of him silently. I've tried over the years as he's gained more prominence but haven't been able to yet. The other men I've killed easily. They meant nothing to anyone, an insignificant blip in the world's population. Probably everyone who had come into contact with them was glad they'd disappeared off the Earth.

I continue down Main Street and take a right down Mack Bay Street to the restaurant on the left. It's only been a few days, and I have a special reservation for whenever I want, and I picked today. It helps when one of the owners is the rockstar John Bay and your best friend. Dave is my pretend best bud so I can find out his secrets and use them to my advantage for his demise.

The best restaurants in Bay City have valets and La Nourriture has plenty. I leave my SUV with them and walk Savannah into the restaurant on my arm. This time, her eyes are not wide with fear but with wonder. They inspect everything. Her pink lips part slightly, and the tip of her equally pink tongue emerges. My dick gets hard at the sight of her parted lips, and I picture thrusting between those lips and down her throat. I don't know why I have that sudden thought. She's Dave's wife. I've never thought of her that way before, no matter how gorgeous she is.

My own sexual preferences have become rougher over the years, but I always make sure my partners know what they're getting into. Someone like Savannah would never be able to handle my kinks. My poor wife, she had been killed in a grocery store slaughter and never had to face them because my kinks had started soon after her death. Because of that I've become the butcher of the depraved pedos and rapists, amongst others because he had been arrested but let go due to some bureaucratic inefficiency. I took care of him. He was my first kill. Almost got caught with that one, but learned a lot since then.

The waitress takes us to a table up front but still shrouded in shadows, giving us the illusion of privacy as if we're a couple. I want her to be comfortable. With how submissive she is, she'll make the perfect sub for my dom. I'm sure that's how Dave treats her, but he has it backwards, you're supposed to cherish your sub, not treat her like trash.

A waiter comes to ask for our drink orders, and I order a white wine I think she might like.

"What would you like to eat?" The waiter hands her a menu, she skims and lays it down.

"Whatever you think." Quiet as the mouse I call her.

Her gaze is on her hands folded in her lap. What has this fucker done to this woman to destroy her will? When we go out, Dave says she doesn't feel well or is out with friends to explain her absences. Seeing the way she is now, I'm sure he keeps her isolated from everyone. The perfect slave.

"No likes or dislikes?"

She hesitates for a second, her mouth opens slightly and closes again, shaking her head.

"Did Dave kill any opinion you might ever have?"

Savannah's head jerks up as if yanked by strings, her mouth opens as if to say something but closes again, and she shakes her head.

"No, I have no opinion about anything anymore."

Her voice is so faint I can barely hear the words and the waver of tears she won't let fall, probably, because that would bring another punishment. I hate Dave right now for what he's done to this innocent, sweet woman. Taken everything away from her. Her will. Her intelligence. Everything that was Savannah Holland before she became Savannah Collier.

If I have my way, one day, Dave will pay for his actions. Both as a lawyer getting the deviants off and for what he's done to his wife. I will protect her. Somehow.

CHAPTER THREE

Savannah

I can't remember the last time I laughed, really laughed in enjoyment and not because Dave expected me to. I never knew Conor was so playful. And fun, did I say fun? I couldn't help myself. I let go, no matter the consequences.

Conor wanted to take me home after lunch, but I forgot to tell Dave something about the invoices. If I don't, I know he'll be madder than if I had done what he told me and gone home right after lunch. Conor said he'd wait in the parking lot for me.

When I push on the office door, it's locked. Maybe he left already? It's only been about an hour and a half, so he should still be here. I get my key out and unlock the door, walking inside. I hear sounds from his closed office door, he must have a client in there with him, one wasn't scheduled. I bite the inside of my lip, hesitant. Should I leave a note on the door and get the hell out of here as fast as I can to safety? There is no safety with Dave as my husband. I have nowhere to go, no one to help or save me.

I tip-toe to my desk so I don't disturb them, shuffling through everything until I find my Post-it notes, and I write a quick message about the client and invoice, creeping over to the door and pressing it to the wood, but the door slowly swings open.

Dave's naked, flat ass is the first thing I see. He's pumping fast and hard at a girl leaning on his desk, tears running down her face that is pressed hard on the wood surface. She looks my way, her scared, big brown eyes pleading and talking to me.

"Dave," I gasp. I knew it. That's why he's always out so late at night, not working. Not that I'm not glad I don't have to be around him.

He twists his head around, his cock still in the girl's pussy. And I think girl, she doesn't even look eighteen yet. She starts to lift her body off the desk, but he grabs her by the nape of her neck, pushing her back down. She cries out as he grinds her cheek into the wood, his vicious nature obvious in the black and blue bruising on her body.

I take a step forward to help her, even if my husband has his dick inside her, I can tell she hasn't agreed. Dave turns back to me, he slides out of her, his dick flopping grotesquely, moving toward me, his hand raises to slap my face. It's coming in slow motion, closer and closer, faster and faster, only inches away, the lines on his hand get larger as it rushes toward me.

A hand grabs Dave's wrist in a handcuff like grip, stopping the forward motion. Both Dave and I turn and find Conor is the one holding him prisoner.

"What the fuck?" he snarls, his face scrunched and teeth exposed, red like a demon.

"Dave, let that poor girl go and pull yourself together, man." Conor's face upshifts into blinding fury.

Dave groans at the agony of his wrist as Conor's grip is crushing, swiping at Conor's fist with his other hand, ridiculous-looking with his pants pooling around his feet.

Conor throws Dave's arm away, disgust in every tight, hard line of his body. Dave scrambles to pull his pants up, releasing the girl who stumbles out of his reach.

"What the fuck, Conor?" he screams, glaring and rubbing his wrist.

I can see a red welt forming around his wrist, holding it close against his body.

"You're asking me?" Conor growls back, his growling tone as low and threatening as a tiger ready to pounce. "What the fuck are you doing? Are you insane? Attacking your wife and this girl? Is she even over eighteen? She doesn't look like she agreed." He waves his arm between us, stopping on the girl who's trying to put her clothes back together, shoving fearful stares at both men.

Dave's gaze jabs at me, blaming me, as if he's stabbing me with a stiletto knife, slicing deep into my abdomen. His eyes promise retribution later.

"What are you doing, Conor? She's agreeable. Right?" Dave glares at the young girl, daring her to disagree. He turns that same look on Conor. "You do know who I'm becoming, right? I'm going for the senate in California."

Conor rolls his eyes, moving closer, to loom over my husband. "I don't care, Dave. A pedophile is a rapist. If she says no, it's no."

"She agreed. Riigghht?" Dave's hard face and voice dares the girl to disagree.

I know what will happen if she disagrees, and I can tell by her body language she wants to. His lips transform into a grotesque version of what he thinks must be a sexy, provocative smile he must think will turn her on when all it does is make her more scared.

"Sure, yes, I did," she blurts out fast in a tiny voice, hurrying steps to take her as far away from my husband as possible.

I understand her and wish I can do the same, but I have to go home to him. If he's going to blame me for this disaster, I can only imagine what he will do to me later. Actually, I can't. It's never been this bad before. Will he kill me? He can't, what would he do with my body? And what is this about the senate?

"See, she agreed. Are we done?" He tucks his shirt back into his slacks and straightens the waistband, the clicks of him fastening his belt are loud in the silent room, except for the girl's panicked pants.

"Nowhere near being done, Dave," Conor growls. "But for now. Just watch yourself, I'll be watching you."

"Is that a threat?" Dave bursts out laughing, dramatically bending over as if he's doing a belly laugh, his blue eyes as hard and clear as ice chips.

"Threat? No, nothing like that." Conor's black eyes are obsidian, no emotion crosses through the dark depths, as deep and dark as the fathoms of the deep seas, no light penetrates the frigid abyss.

"Great, then I'll take my girl home." Dave holds his hand out for me to take.

I scurry back toward Conor. Dave's mouth flattens into a straight line, and my heart becomes a heavy lump in my chest. Oh, God. I did it now. I wasn't thinking, only reacting. Stupid. Stupid. I'm never to show my fear to others because it shows him in a bad light.

He'll kill me for sure now.

CHAPTER FOUR

Savannah

My hands shake as I pull the chicken and vegetable casserole out of the oven, setting it on the stove top. I can't help stopping every few seconds to listen for his car. I'm not allowed to drive, except to the grocery store for exactly one hour, and then I can't leave again until the next trip.

I wash my hands in the sink, my head turns to the window, my eyes plastered on the driveway, waiting for the sight of Mercedes SUV headlights turning into our drive. I'm not sure what his punishment will be. Probably the worst he's ever done or some new discipline for sadism he's researched.

The things I witnessed today turn my stomach like a fan on high. What he was doing to that girl. When Conor asked if she was eighteen, she had turned white. She said she just wanted to go home, so Conor took her there and told her to be careful from now on, she was too young for her life to be ruined this way.

She whispered to me, "I thought he was so handsome and distinguished and surprised he was so interested in me." If she only knew his white teeth were veneers and his full head of hair was plugs. I hope she listens to what Conor told her and be careful from now on who she goes home with.

I get back to what I was doing, covering the casserole and putting the oven on warm. I shake my head, my stomach churning enough for me to feel sick. All I can do is hope he's not too late. I'd hate to find out what he'd do if dinner was dried out.

Standing, I'm shocked his car has parked in the time it took me to reach into the oven.

My whole body trembles, and I hurry to get his glass of wine ready, hoping this might make his mood better. The shaking of my hands makes the wine swirl and spill over the top as I pour. Shit. I grab a towel and stab at the liquid, glancing over my shoulder every few seconds, my heart like a caged bird bashing against the bars, despite them being electrified. Hoping to get everything perfect before he walks in the door.

His pounding footsteps knell the coming stripping of myself the closer he gets. I bite my bottom lip so hard I taste blood. I raise my shoulders to the bottom of my skull, even though I know I can't protect myself. I fight the tears wanting to release the tension of waiting. The footsteps end, and my soul shrivels into a stamp-sized envelope.

"Where's dinner?" His voice is mild and calm, but I don't trust it.

After eighteen years of marriage, I know that calm and mild are when he's at his worst.

"I...I've got it all ready." I try to not stumble over my words. He hates it when I show emotion.

I pick up his plate from the table, not daring to look at him because if I do, I might start screaming. He gets this demonic expression where his blue eyes get so dark they're almost as black as Conor's. Now, his black eyes can appear warm and suck me into him, his very human soul, which can be warm or cold as the highest elevations on the planet.

I trip over something, and the plate filled with food crashes to the floor. Chicken, white sauce, and vegetables splatter in a wide pattern. I gaze down to find Dave's large foot, outstretched in a deliberate move to trip me. His lips stretch in joyous pride at what he did.

"You made a mess, Savannah. I think you should clean it up. Don't you?"

Reasonable tone. I shake trying to control my voice to be as steady as can be.

"You stuck your foot out so I'd trip." I wince at my stupidity. Should think before I speak. Why do I never do that anymore?

"Talking back to me? Really, wife?"

My eyes flash back down to the floor, back down to the splatter. The bottom of his chair grates along the floor, and I blanch, cowering as I wait for what I know is coming. The flesh of his palm slaps on the nape of my neck, pushing slowly down to the floor. Down onto my knees, down until my face is barely an inch above the surface.

"Clean it."

"H...how? Y...you have to let me go." My hands are flat on the tile, just keeping my upper body away from the sharp edges of the ceramic and smashed food, my knees not so lucky as sharp edges pierce into the legs of my pantsuit.

"No, no, no," he drawls, his tone even more reasonable. I quake inside. "You need to clean this mess up with your mouth. Eat it."

My brain paralyzes for an instant, stupefied by his order. I stare down at the jumble of food and slivers of the plate. There's no way to separate the two. His hand pushes harder on my neck, and I repel him as hard as I can. I'm starting to lose, not strong enough in this position. Not strong enough at all. Dave might be slender, but he works out and is strong. Not as strong as Conor, God, I wish he was here. That's a wish that won't come true, he can't save me. No one can.

"Go on. Clean your mess up, baby."

My lips are barely above the slop now. "The glass. I can't eat that." The floor is kept exquisitely clean, but it's still been walked on. I hate it when he calls me a pet name. I push my lips together as they touch a sharp piece that pierces my bottom lip. The jagged spark of pain makes the plight I'm in even more disturbing. I release the floor with one hand slapping at his arm.

"Yes, you can, baby. That's part of the mess you made, so you have to clean it up."

He pushes me further, and I touch the now cold food, a crash sounds, and thundering beats against the floor. Dave's hand leaves my neck, and a threatening growl echoes through the kitchen. I lift and turn my now free head.

Conor stands over us, an avenging angel or a demon. I'm unsure. His black eyes burn with an otherworldly fire, red flames rise in the depths, a rage so deep, so dark, it's like a black hole, except for the little bit of red. Conor has Dave by the shoulder, towering over him, fingers biting deep into the cloth of his shirt. That will bruise. See how he likes it.

Teeth lift over his lips in a snarl, and Conor continues to growl, "What are you doing to her? Do you want to die?"

CHAPTER FIVE

Conor

"What are you doing to her? Do you want to die?" I ask my former best friend.

I've been watching the house ever since I dropped Savannah off, knowing Dave would be up to no fucking good when he got home. I knew he would put everything on Savannah, that's what narcissists do. I was standing outside when I heard the crash and her scream.

I dig my fingers deeper into his shoulder until he lets her go, his mouth twists both in agony and distaste at my touch. He's also OCD about being touched and has a bit of psychopathy in him, maybe more than a bit. That's why he thinks he'd be a great politician, and he might be, he has no empathy for anyone. He only loves himself.

Once Savannah married him, he got bored. His trail of used women is sickening. So far, over the years, none of them have reported him for any abuse, he must pay well and use an NDA.

"What are you doing in my house?" Dave snarls the words even as I dig harder into his flesh, reveling in his torture. He throws his head back, tossing glares and hisses at the pain he deserves for what he's planned for his wife.

"Protecting your wife."

"If you want the worthless slut, then take her. She's nothing, can't do anything right."

He tries to escape my clutch but can't. Dave might think he's some kind of athletic poser, but he's just that. A poser. Sure, he goes to the gym and works out to keep his manly figure. Ha. I have a home gym and run early in the morning and work out before I leave for the station.

I let him go, his sneer of distaste at Savannah is enough to want to get her out of here and away from him. He climbs awkwardly to his feet, shooting me another glare, and I know he wants to massage the shoulder and wrist I mauled but doesn't dare. He'd lose more face.

"Get the fuck out!" he screams at Savannah; he raises an arm to her, and I clear my throat, reminding him to not even think of it.

She backs away from both of us, her face white as if she might pass out. She turns and runs out of the room and upstairs. She must be getting necessities.

"You know she's not that great a fuck. Fat cunt that she is." Dave leans back against the counter, crossing his arms carefully over his chest.

Knowing how much pain he is in makes me smirk. I would love to cause him more, but I need to get Savannah out of here. I'll take her to my home where I can watch her and make sure she's safe. I have a lot of friends in security who can watch the house. Armed security.

"That's how you talk about your wife?" The nerve of this man; that's his narcissism coming out. He's had this toy for eighteen years and is finally tired of it. He considers her used up now.

He shrugs the good shoulder I didn't maul. "She is obviously infertile. I'll need to get one younger. Where should I send the divorce papers?"

"My place, for now."

Dave chuckles. "That's what I figured. Always after my used goods."

I swallow down the vitriol I want to hurl at him, holding back because I know it will give him more ammunition, and he doesn't need that, being the psychopathic attorney he is.

I push one hand behind my back, curling it into a fist with the effort, trying to appear civil while I wait for her. I turn away from him, not understanding how we could have been friends for as long as we were, even fake friends. Sure, the last ten years or so we haven't been as friendly as we were in the beginning, even though I could tell there was something wrong with him. I didn't know how bad he was back in the early days. Now I do, I don't want to have anything to do with him unless it's to abuse and torture him like he has Savannah.

"I'm ready." She stands with an old fabric bag stuffed full. She must have been ready and thinking about this for a while, she got it ready so fast. Her face is trusting as she gazes at me, innocent trust. She shouldn't. I'm not a good man. I'm dark with a black soul.

"You fuck..." Dave starts and stops when he sees the look of potential destruction on my face.

I will destroy him if he tries anything. He knows I will.

"Let's go." I take Savannah's bag, hanging it over my shoulder, and take her hand in mine. I lead her out of what was her home for eighteen years, one eye on Dave, waiting for him to try something if he's stupid enough. He might be if his possessive anger gets a hold of him and takes over control.

We walk to my car, her body stiff, head held high, eyes constantly moving as if waiting to make sure she's not attacked. She never will again if I have anything to do with it.

I toss her bag in the rear of my SUV and turn to help her in, but she's already taken care of that. She won't be doing that in the future, taking care of herself. It'll be my job until she decides what she wants to do with her life. I'll put in for leave so I can get her situated and used to a life of not being a slave.

She needs to learn to be her own person and not an extension of Dave. It'll take time because I don't know exactly what she's gone through, it'll be up to her to tell me if she wants. I can imagine, I've seen enough unhinged and disturbing things in my line of work. I'll help her get any therapy if she wants that. I know people.

I start my car, leaving her alone to her thoughts. It must be hard for her, starting a new life with basically a stranger. I sneak glances at her, her statue-like stance something I'm not used to, and it makes me uncomfortable and itchy. My brain and nerves itch, I wish there was some way to scratch the feelings away. Dave won't get another opportunity to provoke, rattle, degrade, and debase her.

That won't happen. I will destroy him first.

Whatever it takes.

CHAPTER SIX

Savannah

As we drive up Conor's driveway, my jaw drops, along with my heart. Bright lights surround and highlight a mansion fit for a multi-millionaire. How can he live here? I thought he was a detective. I thought he was a good man. Unless he is a fake and got all this by illegal means like Dave.

I shudder, my skin crawls, afraid I might be in the clutches of a man worse than my husband, if that's possible. I shoot side glances for any inkling Conor is like Dave at all. He could be more of a psychopath than him and hide it from everyone, I don't know if he has any family. I remember Dave mentioning a wife that had died. Maybe he killed her.

Conor seems normal, pressing a button to open the iron gates, not paying me any attention as he drives up the long driveway. It's like something out of a historical romance. He stops and parks in front of the gothic mansion sporting turrets and balconies and everything. Maybe this is someone else's home, and he needs something from here. That's it.

"Whose place is this?" There, I asked.

"It's mine." Well, there went that theory. Now I'm back to wondering how he can afford something like this. It's got to be at least ten bedrooms.

"How?"

"My great grandfather had it built. I inherited it. He invested well, even if he was only a cop." He shrugs a shoulder, his face and the back of his neck turning red. "I don't bring many people here because they think the same thing I know you are right now. I'm not crooked."

"How can you afford the taxes and upkeep? It must cost a fortune." I'm in awe of this place. I want to see what it looks like out the back. "How large *is* the property?"

He lays both hands on the top of the steering wheel, not looking at me, putting all of his attention on the wheel as if it's the most important thing, not what we're discussing. "I have an inheritance that keeps getting interest. I don't use it much, only when I need to, so how much I make as a detective doesn't matter. And it's ten acres."

Wow. I can't imagine how much this property is worth in Bay City. I can see a shred of Bay Lake behind the house, craning my neck a little to catch more of a look as it glows black under the bright moon. I've always loved old houses but never get to see them except restoration shows on TV. I jump out of the car, eager to see the inside.

It looks like a castle from a fairy tale out here. I wonder how original the interior is.

"You're supposed to wait for me to open the door for you." I turn my head at his voice beside me.

"Why? I can get out myself." Does he think I'm old and need assistance? He's at least forty-five, maybe fifty, maybe older by all the gray in his short hair and stubble. But he is built. Tall, six-four, six-five. Muscles forever. I mean, how can he move with those muscles, and the bulging veins visible in his hands and arms should be illegal. I have to remind myself I'm still married, even if my husband is a cheating bastard. I won't be like him. I won't.

I bite the inside of my cheek; I can't help my gaze running leisurely over him from the top of his buzzed, dirty blond hair to the heavy work boots he wears with jeans hugging his lower body any woman, whether a teenager or one hundred and twenty, would have a hard on for. So to speak.

"Take a picture." I throw my gaze up to his smirking face, his jawline as sharp as it was when I first met him when I was eighteen. The tiny wrinkles around his eyes and mouth only make him more attractive. Heat rises throughout my body, the hottest being my face.

"I know you can do it yourself. Did Dave or your previous boyfriends never do that?" he continues, a serious expression drops off his face with downturned eyebrows.

I crinkle my face at him. "No, Dave never has."

"Well, that's his loss." He holds a hand out, and I stare at it as if it's attached to an alien.

I'm already out of the car, his hand holding steady. Waiting. I do one more go, gazing from his smirking face to his hand, and slowly take it. I know he held my hand before but for some reason this feels different. His palm is warm against mine, tingles zap up and down my arm. He curls his fingers, and I do the same. Holding hands is a new concept for me. Dave would grab my elbow or waist, or seize my shoulder, fingers biting in if he was mad and wanted to make a point. Otherwise, he'd never touch me.

His smirk grows to a smile, warming me like Dave's never did. I don't know why I never noticed. Because I was too young, I guess. Dave's eyes never lightened like Conor's do when he looks at me. Dave's are always hollow, soulless, and devoid of life.

A phone rings, and since I don't have one, it has to be his. He searches his pockets and pulls it out.

"Yes?"

I stroll away, not wanting him to think I'm going to listen in.

"Yeah, okay. I'll check on it in a bit. Thanks, Reel." Or that's what it sounds like he said. Yes, I did listen in.

"Let's get you inside. I've got to go, something's come up. Go ahead and look for a room upstairs." He opens the front door with his palm on a pad. "My room is the first on the left. Pick any of the others. Doesn't matter which one."

I walk in first, my eyes wide as I gaze around the cathedral ceiling flying up to the three-story ceiling. An ancient stained glass window on each side of the door. This place is beyond amazing, and I've barely walked through the door.

"I'll get your bag." Conor says, walking back outside to his car.

He told me to find a room, and I'll do that right now while he's busy. I run up the stairs to the second floor, excited for the first time in a long, long while. I find two doors to the left, one on each side of the hallway. Which one? I pick the right, open the door, and fall in love the second I step inside. I don't care if it's right across from his. This is mine.

The room is large enough to have a sitting area. The floor is a pale wood, with a white carpet peeking from under the queen-sized bed. The comforter is a pale yellow with sheets a sunflower pattern. The walls a brighter yellow.

Toeing my shoes off, I step onto the white rug, my feet sinking deep into the softness, toes relish, curling into the downy softness. I walk over to the bed and lay on it. It's like sleeping on a cloud, I can't wait to shower and get into my night clothes.

"I knew you'd pick this room." Conor plops my bag on the floor beside where I'm lying.

My arms and legs spread out like a starfish. "How?"

"It is the most girlish room, and that's how I see you. Dave has made you incomplete. He took that away from you. You have never taken care of yourself. Never paid your own bills?" He raises an eyebrow at me, and I shake my head.

I finish the thought for him. "No, I've never lived on my own, he always bought my clothes, told me where to work. He told me everything to do, I never got to make my own decisions."

"That's what I'll help you with. How to make your own decisions. Do all the things you never got to do."

"Go on vacation where *I* want to go? Live where and how I want?"

My chest and lungs tighten like a screw at the thought of being on my own for the first time. I went from my parents at graduation to marrying Dave the next day. I never got to do anything on my own. Now Conor will help me figure all that out. My eyes shine with the unshed tears I can feel and not see. I am so grateful for this man right now, I will do anything for him.

CHAPTER SEVEN

Conor

Savannah is staring at me as if the thought of learning to take care of herself is a new concept. And it really is. She's never had to, even at the age of thirty-five. Dave has always had that control.

She's going to need security, and I have a couple of men coming over to watch the place tonight. One will be inside in the security control room and the other outside. I have cameras everywhere, inside and out. There's no way anyone can get inside without one of them picking it up while I'm gone. I'll have more come tomorrow.

I hate leaving her alone on her first night here, but I've got a lead on a target, and I have to take it. This animal with one of the cartels killed a family. Husband, wife, four-year-old, and newborn. This is what I do at night, bring justice to the wronged. I have a hacker I found on the dark web, and he finds the information I'm looking for. Namely where these fuckers are hiding.

Reel is his codename. I have him on a secret payroll I send to an offshore account, and he's worth every penny.

I leave her to get herself set up for the night, with some cash in case she wants to order food.

It takes at least an hour to get close to the address I have to Manuel Ortega hiding in East L.A. He's with the Ortega Cartel, related to them as a third or fourth cousin.

This brings back memories when my parents and baby sister were murdered while I was deployed overseas. I didn't find out about it for a couple weeks after, some kind of snafu with the military information. By the time I was allowed to go home, nothing had come of the local police procedures.

Reel got me a deserted house address I can park in front of a couple blocks away with no cameras. I drove my seventies Dodge Ram truck I bought when I graduated high school and just before I joined the Marines. I have fake plates on it, and it's run down-looking enough to fit in this run down neighborhood. I lug my duffle bag over my shoulder, all necessary murder equipment inside. I walk down the street at a slow pace. Not hurrying. Looking around as if I'm definitely not in a hurry. There is a tracker in the duffle for Reel to know where I am and to shut off any cameras before I get close enough. After I leave, he'll turn them back on.

As I meander down the street, my thoughts center around the woman I've been stalking in both my mind and actuality. Excitement and thirst for this shit makes me hard as a rock in my jeans. I live for the exhilaration of stalking these monsters. I'm a monster myself, but not this kind. I don't hurt children or women…well, unless they ask me to, and some do. All I want to do right now is take the edge off by rubbing one off. Can't do that in a neighborhood like this, don't need to get arrested, besides, I'm low on time.

A few months ago, when I met Dave at a club, he mentioned something about Savannah, which got my hackles up in disgust.

He called her a lazy cunt, fat, sexless, barren, and on from there, downgrading his wife, when he's the problem all along.

That's when I started stalking the house. I even went so far as to take a day off work and go up to the house when I knew she was home alone, asking if I could get her out of there.

She opened the door, only a crack enough to see one eye and a sliver of her face. The green eye opened wide as she recognized me.

"Savannah, let me help you get away from him. I know he's abusing you," I begged her.

A bunch of different emotions erupted over her face in seconds. Terror, fear, and back to terror and suspicion. She didn't trust me. I could understand that.

"I don't know what you're talking about. Dave is perfect to me. You can tell him I said I'm perfectly happy and love him." She started to slam the door, but I stuffed my big foot in the way, leaning my forearm onto the side of the house, hovering my greater height over her. Not to scare her more, to show her how serious I was.

"He doesn't know I'm here. I want to help you," I insisted, forcing the words out past my clenching teeth. I didn't know how to convince her.

"Thank you. Tell him I'm fine. We're done here." She stared up at me, not saying anything. There was nothing more I could do, and I took my foot out and stepped back. The door slammed, and I stood alone in front of the closed door feeling more alone than I had in years. There was this yearning I had never had for a woman before, not even my wife. I wanted Savannah safe and away from Dave.

That's when my stalking went into overdrive. I would sit in my old truck a few houses away, smoking cig after cig, flooding the interior with the stink of cancerous smoke. I'd go home in the early hours to sleep a few and go to work, going back to my stalking after.

Now I have another reason to stalk. A sicko who killed a family. Raped the wife multiple times in multiple ways before he killed them. The information the cops found at the time was they raped her in her vagina and sodomized her, slit his throat, then hers, and the two kids right after.

That gives me an idea for him, but I don't have the time to spend torturing him. I need to get in, get business done, and leave. He's the last one in the group of thugs I've taken care of, and he knows it. That's why he's hiding in the darkest corner of East L.A. he can, where only the deepest, depraved sinners of the underbelly of the world burrow.

Reel has another for me in Nevada I want to get to as soon as I can. This one kidnapped two sister preteens, and I don't even want to remember what I read he did to them. Reel says I can take time with him, carve him up into tiny pieces and feed them to the hogs on the farm we'll be staying at. It'll be a resort he never imagined.

I stop at the house just before Manuel's shack, I tug the earpiece out of a pocket and plug it into my ear. "Can you hear me, Reel?" My voice is a whisper of wind, so slight no one else can hear.

"Loud and clear. His cameras are off, as well as the ones across the street and on each side. I'm surprised they can afford them with the way the neighborhood is run down, but maybe that's the way they like it. Makes thieves think there's nothing worth stealing. Mask time." His voice is soft in my ear, so deep a bass you can barely hear it. I've never met Reel and only spoke to him over the phone.

I unzip a portion of the bag and pull out a white mask, it's ghost-like with red horns, pretty simple. Reel knew a guy who would make it no questions and forget about it. I cover my head with the mask, the eyeholes and mouth hole doesn't restrict sight or breathing in any way, and I tuck the extra material into my hoodie, pulling the hood up to further cover my head.

My gun is tucked into the back of my jeans, I also have a knife strapped under my arm for easy get to. Last I pull my durable gloves on, hiding the bag under some dead bushes and tall, dry grass.

Crouching down, even though the cameras are off, I still don't want to be seen and have him shoot me or take off. Taking step by carefully placed step, I move closer and reach a window partially covered by a drape that's caught on something, and I can see inside.

From where I'm standing, there is a grungy living room with furniture that must have been dragged from a trash heap. Manuel Ortega has been dumped from his cartel and family. I wonder what else he's done to have sunk so low to be here. I'd like to send his familia a thank you card.

I don't see him, but he could be anywhere, in another room or not even here. I position the mouthpiece closer. "I don't see him, Reel. Is he here?"

"He's there. He was on messages about ten minutes ago, and it showed this address. He's there somewhere."

"Okay, I'll head in and start searching. Anything else I should know first?"

"Na. I do know you should hurry it up. He ordered a prostitute he uses, and she'll be there within the hour." I drop my head for a second and grit my teeth. Now he tells me.

Tromping through the unkept tall grass silently is extremely difficult, but I make it to the cracked concrete pavers making up the walkway to the front door. I take out my lock picks and prepare to start unlocking the door when it swings open on silent hinges.

This can't be good.

CHAPTER EIGHT

Conor

The door opening on its own can't be a good omen. The creak of it would have brought him out unless he is on the drugs he sells. Is he alive? Does he know I'm here? Questions I can't ask Reel because silence is the name of the game, trying to outwit your prey as he tries to outwit you. And he can't, being some drug land drug dealer. He might have the caginess of a stalked animal, that's it.

I reach around to my back, grabbing my gun, holding it out in front with both hands, waiting for someone to jump out at me. So far, silence and nothing greets me.

I check each room, my head partially bouncing in and back cut. I do it again, walking in carefully, my head tilts to the side as I listen carefully for anything. Anything that can give someone's presence away. Silence still. The only sounds are my slight puffs of air.

Each room reveals nothing. I come to the final room, the kitchen, and check it to find it splattered with blood from one end to the other as if a violent fight happened.

Sprawled face down must be Manuel trying to get to the door and escape. He obviously didn't make it. He's sprawled lying on his front, arms and legs spread eagled. He's wearing no shirt, and it looks like someone took a knife to him, not just knifing him but flaying the skin off his body. Flaps of skin lie around him as if he got away and tried to escape.

Good for whoever did this, wish I had been able to. Sirens off in the distance turns my head in the direction they're coming from. Time for me to leave. "Reel, problem."

"I see. Hold on. Go out front and get your equipment, by that time, I'll know if they're coming for you. What happened?"

"I'll tell you after I'm out of here." I run back the way I came in, grab my bag, and head to the street.

"They're headed there, so run as far as you can to get to your truck. I'll tell you when to stop and walk." His voice is hurried and yet unemotional, something I need right now to get through this. These aren't the police from my force, but if I get caught, that's it for me. They'll find the mask, my bag with all my go to murder equipment. Flaying knives, yes I've done that, duct tape, rope, everything else I could possibly need.

"Slow down. Lower your head, if your mask isn't off, take it off. You're getting close to your car. Look normal. As normal as a brute like you can."

There's the dry humor I'm used to and need to ground me. He's right, I am a brute in more ways than one.

I make it to my truck and toss the black bag in the back seat as if it weighs nothing, and to me, it doesn't; compared to the weights I lift, it is nothing. I start the truck, giving a quick glance over my shoulder, making sure no one is coming. I pull out onto the street, not wanting to look guilty. When I took my mask off, I switched it for a baseball cap and pull it further down over my face. As I pass the cop cars, I slide a glance at them, but they're not paying me any attention. I leave the street and take a roundabout way back to Bay City. There's no way they can connect me to that, so I'm not worried. I'm going to have to put off Vegas for a few and stay off any radar.

Stay home, make sure Savannah is safe, and I'm sure she needs clothes and feminine stuff. "Make it safe?" A voice inquires in my ear, and I jerk, realizing I still have the headset on.

"Yeah, headed back in a slow way. Taking 101. You know what that traffic is like."

"No, since I don't live anywhere near Los Angeles or Cali." Reel's dry response makes me chuckle, relief in every nerve ending and stomach twisting moment. Glad it's over, except I live for these nerve ending and stomach twisting moments. The job doesn't give me enough of them, I should move to more dangerous cities in the county, but I was born in Bay City.

My dick is still hard and not going to go down soon until I take care of it. That will have to happen later. Right now, I have to head home.

"Going to go home and get some, you said?"

I hear a laugh in his bland tone, did I say that out loud? I wasn't even thinking how I wanted to fuck Savannah.

"Go home and bust a nut. Or two, she probably hasn't had a good fucking in a while, so anything you can give her ought to do it."

"Thanks for your help, Reel, but I don't need advice on how to fuck. Good night. Send me a bill."

"Sure, dude, when you do need help, just call. I'm sure I can give you some pointers." The laughter in his voice isn't being held back, and I disconnect from him. I shake my head at him, even though he's gone now. He gives me a hard time sometimes, but he's a good guy. Helped me a lot through all this. Revenge is a hard game to do alone, his advice has helped me a lot. I call him a friend, I'm not sure we're in the same state or even the same country. We've known each other for at least ten years now, maybe more, we've got a lot in common in our goals.

It only takes me about an hour to get back to my home, it's late enough that traffic was lighter. Knowing the object of my new obsession is inside my home makes my dick hard again. I know I can't fuck her yet, knowing she's there is all I need right now. I don't know how traumatized she is, she might never want to have sex again. I'll have to see.

I walk through the door to a silent house. It usually is, but now there are two other people here. I spoke with the other guard outside for a few, and he said everything was quiet. No one tried to get in. I think it's only a matter of time before he tries to get her back, he'll need someone to feed his narcissistic nature as I think he considers her his perfect masterpiece.

First, I go into the security control room I have for all my cameras on all the property and talk with Dan the tech guy, and we discuss how quiet it has been. He agrees with me it's just the quiet before the hurricane that will hit us soon.

I walk up the stairs, glancing at my watch, and see it's just after one in the morning. Too late to knock on her door to see how she's doing. I open the door to my room to find a sleeping beauty in my bed, taking a deep breath, unsure as to what to do now. Letting it out quickly, I walk over, laying my hand on her shoulder, shaking her a little.

She doesn't wake up right away, only mumbles and turns to her other side. I shake her other shoulder, my chest tightening as to why she's here.

Savannah turns onto her back, her shining green eyes open sleepily as she swipes at her face up and down. "Wha...a...t?"

"You must have made a mistake and come to my bed." I give her an out because she must have made a mistake. Why else would she be in my room, but my dick isn't getting the message and rubs against the zipper, getting larger and harder.

"Conor?" She turns her head for a second, trying to remember everything which happened, and puffs out a breath of air. "I got scared. Came to see if you were here yet. You weren't, I just felt so comfortable and just wanted to lay down for a minute. I felt so safe. Must have fallen asleep."

My throat starts to close when she throws the blankets away, and she's dressed in tiny shorts and a tiny shirt.

My mouth opens and closes, no sound escapes as I can't breathe now.

Clearing my throat, I try again. "Yeah, probably best if you went back to your room."

Her cheeks and throat turn red. "I know. I'm damaged goods. No one will ever want me."

She goes to slide out the bed, and I grab her by her chin. "Why would you say that?"

She tries to lower her eyes and not meet mine. "That's what Dave always told me. No one will ever want me. I'm a failure as a woman."

"Failure?" I have no idea of what even to say to that. Flabbergasted isn't even close to what I'm feeling. Insulted for her. Insulted for me. She gets out of bed and starts to walk away. I grab her hand before she can and yank her close, her chest up against my body.

"Failure? He's the failure as a man to not be able to pleasure his woman. Right?"

She sucks in a sharp breath; her eyes grow larger as she lets her breath out slowly. "He never cared to. Conor. Show me what good sex can be like. Please, I need it. I-I can't stand the thought of him. Can you erase him for now? He kicked me out. I don't consider myself married now. We're separated."

CHAPTER NINE

Savannah

I've only been Dave's servant for years now. He goes to others for sex. I dream sometimes what it could be like if a man wanted me to enjoy it with him. Be a participant not just a Barbie doll he fucks.

I asked Conor to show me what good sex is like. I can't believe I was so bold, but Dave can only be abusive to get off and never cared if I did.

He clears his throat, rumbling and growling deep in his chest. "I can't be gentle, Savvy. It's not in me anymore. I'm a beast, not like Dave, but I like it rough. You have to be sure."

Can I do this? I stare into his dark eyes, now dead of emotion as if afraid I'll see the real him, I can feel him, though. He might be like Dave in some ways. A beast like he says, a monster, but he's not the same. I feel it. Earlier, I wouldn't betray my marriage vows. Now? It's only a matter of time before I'm no longer married at all.

I raise my trembling arms to latch around his neck. "I still want you. Make me feel good, Conor. I think I like it rough now. It's all I've ever known, but it's been so long, I'm not sure."

He lowers his head and kisses me lightly on my lips. His touch sends sparks electrifying throughout my body. The sparks head straight to my nipples and pussy, making it clench in anticipation.

Going completely on instinct, I rub my body against his, feeling the length of his cock pressing up through his jeans. He needs to do something about that or maybe I should. I need this so badly, to feel wanted, deserving of an orgasm. It's been so long since I've had one with a man. Conor is a potent mix of bad and not so bad, if that is even possible. I trust him more than Dave, who I don't trust at all. Conor, on the other hand, doesn't have the pure evil vibe pouring out in slimy trails.

"If you want it, unzip me, baby." His voice is so deep it gives me chills rushing over my skin like a lover's touch, a touch I've never experienced yet. Today? I want that.

My fingers tremble, grabbing the button of his jeans and slipping them through the buttonhole. I seize the slider of the zipper and, one tine at a time, slowly lower it, revealing his black boxer shorts until the slider reaches the bottom. My pussy pulses as I part the zipper and grip the band of his silk shorts in my fingers, lowering them, his gasp of pleasure emboldens me to yank them down past his cock, letting it bob free.

Conor grabs his jeans and boxers together, yanking them down to his ankles before gripping my wrists in a tight hold in one hand, hauling them to his hard-as-nails cock. I hold it in both hands, the length longer than both my hands together and thick enough my fingers don't meet. Is this what a porn star looks like? My mouth waters, wondering what his taste will be.

I lean down, taking him in my mouth, the taste of him everything I can ask for. Not a bad taste, salty from his sweat, and I love salt. Dave taught me how to deep throat the hard way, and I take Conor as far back as I can, he's still not all the way in. I try harder, his head taps against the back of my throat and down further. I wait for him to get angry, he's not all the way in, but instead, he groans.

"So good, baby. You're such a good cock slut."

Why do those words make me proud? Dave always told me how bad I was and forced me harder to make me better. That's what he told me, anyway. I want to do whatever I can for Conor, and if it's taking him further down my throat, I'll give it a try.

I push myself into him harder and further down my throat, trying hard to not gag and throw up. I grip his balls in one hand, playing with them, tugging them like I learned. I feel cold air on my chest and fingers touching and rolling my nipple between them. I can't breathe anyway, and the way Conor is playing with me, I can't draw in any kind of air into my depleted lungs.

He helps me along by pushing his hips deep, one of his hands grips the top of my head, and the other my chin in hard clasps. He pulls out briefly, and I grab for a fast breath before he pushes back in.

"Tap my," he grunts and lets out a long groan, "thigh if it's too much."

He drives even harder into my mouth, and all I can do is hold it open for him to use me for his pleasure. It's not his alone, though, I hold one hand against his hard ass and my other is delving between my own thighs, finding my clit and rubbing as if my life depends upon it. It might be for my sanity. I have to get off before he finishes because I'm not sure he'll let me once he's done. Dave never did. Once he was done, that was it, I was, too.

I try to look up at him from under my eyelashes, tears collect at the corners. It's hard from this position, but his face is tight and feral.

He continues to ram his cock down my throat as far as he can, chasing his orgasm with eyes tightly closed, his mouth open and slack. I work on mine, rubbing and pressing down as hard as I can. We both cry out at the same time, mine is more of a gurgle with his dick down my throat. I can't believe our orgasms were synchronized so well.

He keeps pounding away but slower, his cum fills my mouth and throat, throwing his head back, teeth clenching, he surges down my esophagus in a flood of thick fluid. I shudder, my skin hot enough to fry bacon on with how electrified I am. I can't believe an orgasm is so...so explosive.

Conor releases my head, his hand pets over the top and down my hair, and I move away, not knowing what I should do now.

"Was that too much?" It's so sweet how he worries. "I told you I was rough."

"I needed that. I didn't realize. Um." I don't want him to think I'm stupid or silly, he wants to know. I blurt the rest of my sentence out. "An orgasm could be like that. That sex could be so pleasurable and not be totally painful." I gaze down at the floor; afraid he thinks I'm some kind of noob or something.

My hands are grabbed into one of his and he lifts my chin with his other. "That's because he has no feelings for anyone else but himself. Mentally and physically, he cannot think of anyone else's feelings."

I don't think my heart can swell any bigger than it is without bursting into billions of pieces. This man can pretend he is bad, and he might be. I really don't know much about him, only he was Dave's best friend. Until now. I don't know what he's done as a detective for him to think he's a bad man. I know bad men, and he's nothing like Dave, that man is pure evil, and I hope I never have to see him again. I'm sure he'll try to get me back; he needs someone to blame everything on.

"Do you want to go back to your room now?" The question startles me for a minute, my gaze slams onto his, and I can't process what he asked.

"Do you want me to leave? I can if you want." I won't stay if he doesn't want me. Dave and I had separate rooms, he said I snored.

"No, no, I don't want you to think I meant that. You can spend the night here with me if you'd rather. I don't mind, or I can go to another room."

This man thinks he's bad?

"I'd rather stay with you. I'll feel safer." I've never really slept with anyone before. There's so much I'm learning with Conor. I wait for his answer, my stomach and heart churn with the indecision washing over me.

"No problem, here, get back in." His eyes stroke over my body as if he's touching me, it's almost as if his fingers trail over my skin. Those dark eyes of his brush over my breasts, down over my round belly, and further down.

I've never had anyone admire me like Conor is. Like he desires me, lusts. I want more of him, I want all of him, but I'm too scared of putting myself out there. My husband killed any self-confidence I had soon after we married. I can't even remember if I had any.

My parents encouraged me to marry him right out of high school, they didn't see any reason for me to go to university. I was a girl, after all, not the boy they wanted. They wanted me to do exactly what my mother did, and Dave came on scene. Like the young girl from yesterday, I thought he was a good catch, a great man to be seen with and marry. He did everything right to reel me in like a fish on a hook. Thought I was so lucky to get a man like him. Older, accomplished. I was so naïve. So stupid. Not anymore, I'm not.

Conor holds the covers up for me to crawl in and lays them over me to my neck.

"I'll leave my boxers on. I don't wear pajamas."

All I can do is nod like an idiot, he walks over to the wall and shuts the light off. A pale night light goes on, and I hear the shuffling of clothes and can only imagine him taking them off. I only saw his cock and thick thighs and would like to see more. Sooner rather than later. The bed dips slightly on the far side of me, there's quite a distance between us. I've never seen a bed this big, but he's a big guy.

"Night." His voice is husky in the darkness, I don't know if I can stand being in the same bed as him and not try to jump him.

"Night," I answer in the same tone, lying flat on my back, trying to control my breaths. I wonder if he's having the same problems, the same desires are a torrent racing over me.

I don't move, barely breathe. There's a river of what-do-we-do's lying between us, a deluge of maybes and I wants. And the river and deluge race through a Grand Canyon-sized gulf between us.

Can Conor extinguish the emptiness, leaving the huge black hole that keeps filling in a never-ending waterfall of my loneliness?

CHAPTER TEN

Conor

I'm afraid to move, afraid I'll turn into the beast everyone calls me and fuck her like one. I've never been in this position before. The women are intrigued by my size, wondering if I'm this big all over. I only use the ones who can handle me, hiding what I really want to do. I haven't found the right one yet. I'm sure Savannah isn't the one. She's too submissive. Too scared.

Maybe I should go to her bed or one of the others. She's afraid to be alone, I can't leave her. I'll wait until she goes to sleep, then I'll go somewhere else to sleep. Yeah, that's what I'll do.

I turn to my side, facing away from her, regulating my breathing and pretending I'm asleep so she'll feel more comfortable. Sleeping is a luxury for me, something I don't indulge in very often, or not long anyway.

My body is lit with a current like a high voltage electrical tower. A moan is forced out of me by the tightening in my balls, I'm going to come like I never have before. I open my eyes and jackknife up, the early morning sun streams through the blinds, enveloping Savannah in a halo of white light as she goes to town on my dick, her head bobs up and down on me, deep throating. She's sucking me so hard I think she's going to suck my soul through my dick.

I grab her head, my fingers burrow in the hair by her ears, massaging, not hurting. Such a blowjob is a once in a lifetime experience. Mind blowing.

"Baby." Is all I can get out at one time. One word. So, I try again. 'Savannah." My voice is gravel from sleep. I clear my throat. One more time. "Savvy, stop."

I bend down over her, my thumbs tip her chin up, away from my cock, her bright red lips pout at my interruption.

"Why?" Is her only question.

"You took care of me last night, it's my turn to take care of you." The pointer finger of both hands rub against her cheeks, back and forth, rhythmically, soothing, her eyes close, and she relaxes in my hands.

She rubs her cheek into my palm, a kitten searching for a gentle touch. Love. She's never had that like I did. I've researched her over the past couple years, and it seems her parents were apathetic to her. Wanting a boy. They pushed her onto Dave, and she ate his promises of love up like it was the best gourmet meal. He used to brag about that.

I had so much love, and when I lost it, I lost myself. Perhaps I'll find what I lost with her. In her absence of love, she might teach me how to again. I grab her by her waist and pull her up, flipping her onto her back, her head on the pillow. I pull my boxers back up so there's a little protection from my using her like an animal. Maybe we can do that later. Right now, I want to take it slow. Only give her as much as she can stand, and by the way Dave used her, it could be more than I think.

Moving down her body, my fingers slide into the waistband of her tiny shorts, yanking them off her body and pushing her shirt up over her tits. I take her tits in my hands, massaging and flicking over the tips with my fingernails. I bite my bottom lip to keep myself from pulling and twisting them until she cries out in pain.

My upper body slides down so I can start working on her pleasure. I move one arm down, lifting her leg over my shoulder, giving myself more room to work. I burrow my face in her shaved pussy, my tongue flicking over her clit, moving to her opening and going back and forth between the two teasingly. She starts riding my face, her hips humping, searching for release.

Her moans and whimpers are the beautiful music of the night, getting ready for a crescendo with a clash. Her head and body arch, her mouth opens and twists with words and screams unsaid. She's a work of art.

I lift my arm, my middle and ring finger at her mouth. "Open for me, baby."

And she does as I say, like a good girl. I know she's been trained in a horrid manner by Dave, but it's better for me. I don't have to go through all the work.

I bury my fingers inside her mouth, all the way to her throat, I know she can take it. She just did with my dick.

Tears race down her face in rivers as she chokes and gags, sucking with everything she has as I suck on her clit and opening to get everything she has to give.

"You taste so good, Savvy. Such a good girl, sucking cock like you do. Get ready to come." I praise her, barely get two fingers inside her, and she violently shakes her head.

Am I hurting her? I yank my fingers out of both her cunt and mouth. "Am I hurting you?"

She's still shaking her head. "No. No. I want." Her face turns such a beautiful shade of red. "I...I want to have sex with you." She gets the words out in a rush, clearly embarrassed.

"I don't think you're ready yet." I don't want to deny her, but her husband just threw her out yesterday. With the abuse she has endured with him, I don't think it's time yet.

She grabs my hand into both her hands, gazing up at me, pleading. "Conor, I need this. Trust me. All the physical and mental abuse I've been through, I don't consider myself married. For a long time now, I have thought of myself as a prisoner. Chained and shackled with a marriage license and fear. Fear of what he would do to me if I tried to leave. So, please, please do this for me." She releases my hand with one of hers and lays mine against her hot cheek. "I need to feel like a person again. Not a thing. A possession. Do you understand?" Her soft voice is as pleading as her wrinkled brow and face.

How can I say no?

CHAPTER ELEVEN

Savannah

"Do you understand?" I need to feel desired. Not like something to be used and tossed aside until he's ready to play again.

"I want to be sure this *is* what you want. You are still married."

"He tossed me out like trash. We might still be married on paper, but to me, it's over. I'll never go back. Never." I shudder at the thought of being anywhere near him again. I can't even think of seeing his face again. The thought makes me want to vomit.

"I don't want to hurt you; I can be rough. Say red, and I'll stop. I know the word is cliché, it'll work." The furrow in his eyebrows is as deep as the Gulf of Mexico, he's so worried.

"I don't think you can." I want to explain he can't do anything worse than Dave. And I hope it will make me feel alive again. "I think I'm broken. The way you…" I bite my bottom lip, closing my eyes for a second. Dave can't hurt me. I can say or do anything I want and not have to worry. "The way you fucked my throat. I enjoyed it so much. More than anything, so I'm not worried about your being rough and hard. I want you to teach me." There I said it, I know Conor isn't my husband, but there's still this niggling doubt he can suddenly mirror the kind of immoral man Dave is.

He leans closer, our faces almost touching, close enough if I move a half an inch, we'd be kissing. Would that be so bad?

"For me, you're not broken. For me, you're perfect. I can teach you so much, and you will revel in the combination of pleasure and pain. In our world, there's no pleasure without pain. Are you willing?" He takes my face between his hands, holding me as his willing prisoner. I can't move or speak; my eyes must tell him my feelings. His lips crash into mine, our mouths open, a carnal mashing of lips and tongues and teeth, and breaths mingling, and hearts realigning into one.

He's naked now. I don't know when that happened, and his body is *shredded.* He's a mass of muscles and black and colorful tattoos.

Hard, lean muscles cord over his upper body, to his impressive eight-pack clenched with every harsh breath he takes. For a fiftyish-year-old man, he's fiiinnne. Now, his sinfully defined v runs down to the area showcasing his equally impressive cock.

I start to wrap my arms around his neck, but he grabs my wrists in one of his hands, moving them over my head. My adrenaline high crashed along with my orgasm when he abruptly stopped his oral before. His hold on my wrists is so tight, his hand shackles my upper body. I strain to break free, moaning as I pull on my arms, wanting to touch him. Somewhere. Anywhere, and I moan again in my frustration. He chuckles, his hand clamps harder on my wrists, this pain also a pleasure zipping straight to my core. "Not yet." His voice is tires on a gravel road.

He's lying between my legs, and I wrap them around him. I can't believe I'm doing this, I'm dry humping him to get myself off.

Wiggling my lower body against him and his hard cock, I want those feelings back from before he stopped. The swelling heart feeling, tightness in my chest, electrical charges surging to my core, my body tightening like a spring ready to explode. I want that again. I want it now.

His kisses are a fine, decadent wine I can't get enough of.

Conor wrenches his mouth away from mine, his pants are like mine. Deep and desperate for more. He lies on either side of me. He runs his tongue from the top of my chest up the hollow of my throat, where he pulls the skin into his mouth, biting down hard, the sharp bite of pain yanks a gasp out of me. He releases his teeth and sucks hard, and I'm sure he'll leave a mark for everyone to see.

He kisses his way down my chest, living little bites behind him. What kind of screwed up am I that wetness seeps out at each bite. What is wrong with me, something like this turns me on?

Grabbing my nipple into his mouth, he plunges into me, not giving me any kind of notice, but I don't care. He feels so good inside me. Conor slides back out and crashes back in, the force hurts all the way back in, and yet, so damn good. He's so big, his cock hits all the right places inside me. If I only knew sex could be so good. So pleasurable.

He kisses down to my belly, his tongue licking at my belly button, and I wiggle. Who knew it was an erogenous zone. As the head of his dick bumps against my cervix, I shudder as he takes my face in his hands, tipping my face up and back. The breath strangles in my throat as he wraps his hand around my neck and squeezes. He doesn't squeeze too hard, just hard enough for my breath to wheeze. I need him as much as he needs to fuck me. There. I thought the word I've never been allowed to say. And I am going to say it whenever I feel like it. Fuck!

I grab at his shoulders when he hikes one of my legs up around his waist, and he raises one of his legs and kneels on the bed beside us. He thrusts back inside, hard, and I feel him everywhere. He feels like he's in my womb.

This isn't like when Dave was rough when we had sex because that's all it was for me. For him, I think he was proving he owned me as his property. Dave left marks all over my body all the time, I hated, hated, *hated* it. The fingerprint bruises, the lashing marks, the scars.

With Conor, it's different somehow. The marks and pain he leaves behind isn't to hurt or humiliate, it's to indulge me in the new feelings of my own sensuality. Show me what I can become if I let myself.

I hated being with Dave so much I would dream about leaving him. I wanted it so much when he would force me to have sex with him, I'd take a morning-after pill even though I was on birth control. He wanted me to have a baby so he can continue his legacy. No way, so I met a doctor when he would take me to make sure I didn't have any diseases; he knows he was my first. But she saw everything and risked everything to bring me six months worth of birth control during the hour he would let me loose on my own to go grocery shopping.

When she first saw me, she was going to report him, but I begged her not to, saying he would kill me if she did. She agreed reluctantly. Every time I would get down to one month, I'd text her on my old cell phone my parents gave me when I was in high school. It barely works now, and I would wait daily for it to die. I still have it in my bag now.

Conor releases me and flips me over onto my stomach; boy, is he strong, who knew how sexy that is. I raise up onto my hands and knees, but he pushes down between my shoulders until I'm lying flat, my cheek against the sheets, chest flat and ass in the air. He better not be thinking to put that in my ass. He spreads my cheeks, and I wiggle to get away, my hands scrabble at the loose sheets, and I feel a sharp pain that dissolves to desire.

I gaze over my shoulder at him, and he reaches out with his palm, it disappears, and he spanks my pussy again.

"Conor," I cry, tears not only spring, they pour down my face, a thunderstorm not about to end any time soon. I don't know what to think. There's pain, yes. But it hurts so good.

"Do you hate it?" he groans, every time he spanks me, he plays in my wetness with two fingers, spreading it around to my clit and rubbing my nub, and I'm pouring. "Use your words. Tell me. Do. You. Hate. It?"

"No. I love it!" I gasp, he spanks my pussy again, right over my clit, and the pain sparks and jolts straight through me as if I've been electrocuted. My breaths come hard and fast. I suck in a ragged breath, arching my back as he slams into me again. And again. And again. Over and over.

His lips trail down from the nape of my neck, down my spine as far down as he can reach with him still being inside me from behind. I can't seem to get enough from him. Is there something wrong with me, turning to him right after my husband kicks me out of our home? I haven't been in love with him since he started beating me. I don't even know if I actually was in love with him or in love with the idea of being in love.

Now, my heart swells, thinking of Conor and what he's doing to me, how he makes me feel cared for for the first time in my life. I never had that growing up. I was born the wrong sex and was always told I should have been a boy.

A hand falls on my ass, and he spanks that this time. Every time he pushes into me, his hand smacks on my ass, and I get wetter. "Please." My voice sounds as needy as my body, wanting him to keep doing everything he wants to me. There's nothing he's done I haven't liked.

"Please what?" He groans as he slams back into me, more frantic and uneven this time, his heavy, hard balls slap my clit, filled with the cum he wants to fill me with. Fine with me.

"Please, spank me again. Fill me up." I can't believe I'm begging him to use me, to spank me.

His hard hand slaps down as if he's trying to bruise me, and I love it. I revel in the hits; I shiver, wanting more. I'm so sick in the head. I shouldn't enjoy this after what Dave has done to me, should I?

He pumps twice more into me, his hands on my hips, holding himself into my body as his cum fills me, imprisoning me in his grasp. I collapse flat on my stomach, unable to hold myself up anymore, and he lets me, following my body with his, still inside me. He pulls me up against him, his arms holding me tight. This is so good, I've never had this closeness with anyone before, not even my mother. I can learn to like this.

CHAPTER TWELVE

Conor

I walk to my Range Rover, my head down, filled with thoughts of her. Of what we did only an hour ago. I left her sleeping; I've already told her I had to leave for a few days, but men will be there to keep her safe. She's used to following orders and obeying, so there shouldn't be a problem.

Savannah is a special woman and never deserved the life she was given, and in spite of everything, she is the sweetest person I've ever met, besides my mother.

My phone vibrates in my pocket of my jeans, and I dig it out, I look and see it's Dave. *What the fuck?* I think to myself. I debate for a minute whether to ignore the call and decide to find out what he wants. I'm waiting for a call from Reel anyway.

I click accept. "Yeah, what?"

"Is that how you talk to your best friend, Conor?" I hear the superior attitude he always has had talking down to people. He's even had it for his clients, just toned it down some.

I snort. "We've always been fake to each other our whole lives, Dave. At least we can admit it now."

He laughs like he always does when he thinks he has the one up on someone. He might think that he doesn't really know me. I've kept the way I've felt about him silent for years. I've definitely been a fake friend, from the day he brought her to dinner to brag. I don't know for sure, but I think the only reason he married her was to be able to do the kinks he likes on someone who wouldn't fight back. He knew Savvy was too submissively trained by her parents, probably friends with them.

As I listen to Dave's heavy breaths into the phone, I think of my little captive in my bed. Thinking of chasing her in my mask, capturing her, and pushing her into the dirt in the forest on my property. Savaging her the way she likes with my cum in every hole she has. And I mean *every hole.*

"I'm going to get her back, Conor. Any way I can."

"Give it a try. Give it a try. You will never get your slimy hands on her again. I can promise you that." I can't hold back the growl rising up from my chest. He'll know I have feelings for her. I can't help myself.

He laughs in pleasure this time, and I grind my teeth in frustration. I gave him an in to my psyche.

"That didn't take long, my friend." I grunt at his term and continue making my way to my car, wanting to end this call but needing to hear what he has to say and if I can decipher his intentions to Savvy. "Feelings for my little wifey already, huh? She's right up your alley. She just lays there and takes it with her eyes closed."

I think it's time to turn the screw a bit, so he knows who the woman he married actually is. "You really don't know her, *friend*. She's wilder than you think. Guess it takes the right *kind* of man to bring her wild side out. You're not that man."

Pressing the button to click open the door and start the car, I get inside, my murder bag already there. My phone buzzes with an incoming call from Reel, and I need to take it. "Gotta go, friend. We'll talk again." I press the red button on my phone and the green to talk to Reel.

"Everything ready?" I ask, wanting to make sure plane tickets and hotel are taken care of. I'm also going to watch the football game in one of the sports bars to be seen.

"Got it all done. Also know where he's living. He's got a pregnant girlfriend, though."

Not sure what to do with that information. Charlie Norton is a lowlife scumbag who, while excessively drunk, t-boned a car and killed a man and his wife and young daughter. That was ten years ago, and I finally found him; this time, he will suffer for what he did instead of getting off scot-free. I will make him suffer ten-fold for all those years he's lived a life while they didn't. While a thirteen-year-old girl had to die before her time. I don't fucking care if he has a girlfriend, wife, and ten kids for every year he's lived. I will string out his suffering. And mine.

I don't sling a glance back at my home to catch a glimpse of the woman in my bed. I don't fucking care. Not at all. I press hard on the gas pedal and take off fast, cursing the concrete circle driveway that doesn't give me any kind of satisfaction on spraying gravel or anything when I zoom the engine with my right foot, and punching on the clutch with my left. I watch the guard hurry to open the gate as I race out as if on a track.

Charlie doesn't know who's coming for him. It will be a not-so-nice surprise. I'll have to figure out a way to get him away from his pregnant girlfriend.

I race my SUV onto the 10 East to get to the 15. My thoughts race as much as I do weaving in and out of traffic at this later time of the night.

Savvy is a nice surprise of decadent beauty. Her willingness to take us to a next level will make the chase even better as my delicious prey.

What we did earlier was a passion I've never felt before, one of unbridled ferocious hunger and a craving lust which still has me in its grasp. I want to go back right now and fuck her into a stupor. Okay, I might have done that already. I smile to myself, weaving around a slower vehicle and back to the fast lane.

My heart twists and spins dizzyingly as it taps a dance for a sixties dance hop. I bite my bottom lip, wanting to turn around and go back to Bay City, getting into bed with the voluptuous beauty I left sleeping in my bed.

Luckily or unluckily, however you think about it, my phone rings, and I glance at the touchscreen multimedia receiver in my car. It says unknown, but I know who it is. He'll be giving me an update on where Charlie might be. I plan on stalking his home and work out how to get to him. I don't want his girlfriend involved. I don't hurt innocents. And with her being pregnant, that makes her a double no go.

"Reel, what you got for me?"

"Conor, they've disappeared."

I slam on my brakes and swerve over four lanes of traffic onto an exit ramp and into a convenient strip mall and slam the SUV into an empty parking space, barely having heard the roar of horns, squealing brakes, and curses from the other drivers. I'll be lucky if someone doesn't come over and shoot me for that action, the way things are nowadays with road rage.

"What the fucking fuck do you mean disappeared? How can they disappear?" I'm stuck in a black hole of despair and gut-wrenching sorrow at the consequence of it. I can't believe this is happening.

"I don't know. This has never happened to me before. I can follow anyone, and I mean, *anyone*. I don't know…" He trails off, he's never not been able to finish a job before. Never lost someone he's stalked online. Never lost. I can't see his face. I've never met him, but the disappointment in his tone assumingly makes him feel like a failure.

"When did you lose him? You had his whereabouts, what? A half hour ago?" I slam my fist on the steering wheel, wanting to take my disappointment out on something. I'm still going to Vegas; Reel might have something else by the time I get there. I need to get going if I'm going to make it there before morning.

CHAPTER THIRTEEN

Savannah

I wake up to darkness, and I hate the dark. I always leave a nightlight on or the bathroom door open with the light on in there. I never knew when Dave would appear out of the night to attack me. To show me what a *man* he is. He's nothing compared to Conor; now *he* is a man.

I lift myself to my elbow, staring out a slight glimpse of the window. A full wall of windows shows a slight lightening of the sky, so I must have fallen asleep again. Conor's been gone two days so far. I fall onto my back, not wanting to sleep or get up, depressed with how my life is going.

Turning onto my side, I yank the covers up to my neck, huffing at being alone here with nothing to do, no friends to call. Dave made sure of that. I'm having a woe-is-me moment right now, and I'm going to wallow in it.

In the distance, in this house, it's quite a ways, a door slams shut. Is that the front door? The guards don't slam any of the doors, they try to be quiet and be barely seen and not heard.

Footsteps pound on the stairs. Is it him? Did he find me? Why isn't there fighting if it is?

I slither my body over to the other side of the big bed, pouring myself over the side. No, no, I whimper, curling into a ball, wishing I could slide under the bed. This is a platform bed that goes all the way to the floor. Who freakin' has a bed like this? Really?

Twirling my head almost like a top, I search for something to protect myself with. What man doesn't have a bat within reach to protect himself with? Huh? A friggin' muscle-bound giant is who. I squint at the four-foot metal lamp on the other side of the nightstand.

I *will* protect myself. I can do this. My blood pressure spikes to a DefCon One nuclear attack level. Maybe a heart attack level, whichever comes first. The adrenaline rush makes my wide-awake nerves spark with an electrical storm level five. Clutching the lamp tighter between my hands, my fingers turn white with the pressure I'm using.

My pulse ramps with a thump, thump, thump of my heart, in tune to the thud, thud, thud of the footsteps as they get closer. My body shudders with cold blood freezing in my veins.

I stand, lamp in my now cold, still, white fingers, my body shaking everywhere, but I'm resolute to save myself. Not wait for someone else to do it this time.

The doorknob turns ever so slowly, not making a sound. Cold fingers stalk up and down my spine. I watch, my eyes as wide as they can get. The fingers not only grasp my spine, they now hold my heart tight in its grasp.

I watch the door creep open, whoever is opening it is trying to be quiet. It can't be Dave because he wouldn't care if I was scared. In fact, it would thrill him. It's someone else.

Creeping forward, I move closer to the door, standing on the other side, waiting as my hands shake so badly the lamp shakes, for a head to sneak through. I draw a deep breath in, watching as the top of a dark head appears, and I strike, hurling the pole of the lamp down as hard as I can at the head, screaming as the pole falls to the back of his neck.

He turns his head at the same moment, the shrieks alerting him, and it's Conor staring right at me. He heaves his forearm over his head to protect himself, hurling himself at me, grabbing the lamp pole and launching it against the wall. It crashes, leaving a huge hole when it bangs, falling to the floor.

The snarl and dark glint of violence on his face is a promise that is terrifying. This is the beast I should be afraid of, but for some reason, I'm not. This beast brings out something dark within me, something Dave grew and nurtured, something I've hidden so I wouldn't give him a reason to beat me. He is the reason I'm broken with these secret desires I have. Ones breaching the surface as Conor glares. He takes a step forward, and I take one back, my back against the wall, his chest flush against mine.

I inch to the left, the backs of my arms and shoulder blades scrape against the plaster.

He bends down, looming over me, his lips brush against my earlobe. "Little mouse. Little mouse. Trying to escape? Want to run and me to chase?"

I'm distracted by him saying *chase*. Is that what I want? To run and be chased? Caught? My breath catches in my throat at the ideas racing through my head. Am I crazy for considering this? My pulse jams at the thought.

I give him a little nod, and his black eyes gleam hot, his voice growls with darkness, "Little mouse wants me to throw her on the ground and fuck her like an animal?"

The images he reveals makes my eyes close on a moan, and my shorts get wet between my thighs. I think to myself, yes please.

His mouth brushes mine, his breath is my breath. "The guards are gone for the next two hours. The cameras are off. Go, run. Run, little mouse, as fast as you can, but I'll find you and catch you. And fuck you. Run."

I'm wearing my night clothes, pajama shorts and tank top and bare feet, but the snapshot in my mind makes me turn and run. Run like my feet can take flight, down the stairs, out the front door, and cutting through the vegetable garden. I don't dare steal a glance behind me to see how close he is. I can't hear anything other than my harsh, loud breaths. Quiet, I'm not.

The grounds are kept immaculate, but I am still afraid for the soles of my feet running as fast as I am. A quiet crack comes from my left, and I edge more to my right, hoping he's not leading me the way he wants, if he is, there's nothing I can do about it. He'll have me anyway he wants, and I think I'll only pretend to fight.

CHAPTER FOURTEEN

Conor

I grin to myself, my darkness fighting to the surface, self satisfaction in every pore of my body. My pulse rises to rocket speed imagining her flat on the grass, my hand holding her down by the nape of her neck. Her shorts torn from her body, no underwear covering what's now mine. She'll always be mine. She's my new addiction, an addiction I never want rehab for.

She can't go outside the grounds, so there's no reason to hurry. There's rolled barbed wire along the top of the iron barbed fence, and if she tries the gate, there is no way she can get through there, either. All around the property, the fencing is eight feet tall.

I take one long step at a time, my combat boots boom on the landing and steps as I walk down. I'm in no hurry, let her think she can get away, but I know she doesn't really want to. She wants this as much as I do. It's a good thing Dave fucked her up as much as he did because she was too innocent before he got his hands on her. Now she can learn what kinks she likes and dislikes.

The front door is wide open, so unless she's not panicking and did this to deceive and mislead me, this is the way she went. I know she doesn't want to mislead me; I saw the glow from her excitement in her eyes and face. She's looking forward to this. This is probably the most enthusiasm and titillation she's ever had, on a level with her assent.

I make a stop at my Range Rover, opening the door and unzipping my murder bag, pulling out exactly what I want. My mask. This will change everything she thinks will happen; this she won't expect. I slip it on over my head and glance down at the lawn to see where her feet have pressed down on the grass. I follow her dash across there to the vegetable garden, her footprints a road map with precise instructions of where she's headed.

The forest I grew one tiny tree at a time from when I was a kid, knowing this was my legacy. Live oak trees fill an acre of land with bushes and flowers underneath. This is where she's headed. Exactly where I want her to go. I want to take her in the dirt, I want to dirty her pristine appearance. I want to ruin her, except different than the way her husband did. I want her to conquer her fears and vanquish any reminder of what Dave did to her. I want her to come into her own and become a phoenix. Rise above the mouse she was. She'll be more. She will become my queen, whether she knows it or not.

She doesn't realize she's leading me right to her, probably too panic stricken to realize her steps are visible. Or she doesn't care, either way, my dick jumps in time with my heart rate every time I spy another footprint.

Now that I've had a taste of her, I want more, I have a hunger that won't easily be filled. A desire which won't be filled this morning. Won't be filled tonight or tomorrow. I don't think this hunger and darkness will ever be filled. I adjust the throbbing bulge in my jeans and continue my hunt.

My prey is doing well in hiding, the new dawn is helping her. The darkness in the forest is helping her. When full light rises, she won't have the advantage, but I will find her by then.

I have about two hours to do with her whatever I want, and I want a lot. I want her on her knees, tits, ass, and tongue out, asking me to use her. Not in that exact order. Depends upon my mood and attitude.

Intoxicating thoughts aside, my dick is way ahead of what's going to happen. I mean, my cock is so stiff it could punch through steel. I spy a hint of pink among the leaves and branches. Sure, it could be flowers, but I don't think so. I make sure I'm not quiet at all. I want her to hear me, to worry if I'll find her. She knows I will. I always find what I'm hunting. Especially a woman looking to be fucked hard.

I look down, stepping my boot hard on a small branch, on purpose, and the crack makes her jump, and she peers through a hole between the foliage, her eyes widening when she sees I'm looking right at her.

Savannah makes a squeak, disappearing from my sight. She's running.

I follow behind at a slight jog, the crackling of dry leaves and fallen branches deafening beside the wakening birds in the forest, not bothering to run faster. With my longer legs, I have no problem keeping up. I'm not ready to catch her yet. I'm enjoying the hunt, the chase. It sets my blood boiling and surges in anticipation of the destruction of Savvy to come. I'm going to destroy her pussy for anyone else. She's going to forget Dave ever touched her, she'll forget his name.

My mask is what scared her, the thought makes me grin in satisfaction behind it. A superhero-like or an ogre hunting for his mate. Supple branches bend and snap back as I jog past, pursuing her. The scent of the dirt and flowering brush fragrance is heavy in the morning breeze.

The moist ground beneath her feet slowly swells from the impression they made; I can track her no matter how she tries to hide. Aw. There she is, trying to climb a tree. Silly girl.

Her hands and feet scrabble at the rough bark, leaving dark red splatters, which makes my pulse ramp up to heart attack levels that she would try to harm herself like that.

"Savannah." I growl in a low tone, not needing to raise my voice. She stops and turns, her back to the tree she was trying to climb.

"Stay away. He'll-he'll be right here to stop you." She's so cute, trying to appear brave when I know she's trembling in terror. The goosebumps rising on her skin aren't only from the morning chill, and her tight nipples trying to poke through her tank top reveal how turned on she is. She's not quite sure it's me.

I'll let this go on as long as I can and see how far she's willing to go.

CHAPTER FIFTEEN

Savannah

My insides shake worse than my outside. I think the man in this devil or ghost mask is Conor, but I'm not sure. He said there was no one else here, what if a stranger somehow got inside the gates. He could be on his way to his death, I can't allow that.

I open my mouth to scream, the stranger moves faster than I can imagine and has his large hand over my mouth. I swallow thickly.

"Nuh uh." He growls again, his tone so soft and low I can't tell if I know the voice, his teeth raking over my earlobe. It could be Conor, I can't tell. Right now, I don't care. What is wrong with me?

My front is smashing against his, my back pushing hard against the rough bark of the tree I tried to climb. I feel my nipples poking into his chest. My face and the tops of my ears heat with embarrassment. His hand clamps on my shoulder, making sure I don't try to squirm away.

His eyes. His black eyes are as black as his pupils, making him look demon-like, the sclera blinding-white against the darkness.

The way my body reacts to this masked man shames me. Have I become so screwed up in my head by what I went through in my marriage that *any man* will make me desire whatever they want to do to me?

I moan in the same shame and longing as his hand pushes into my pajama shorts, his fingers swishing through my pouring wetness. The humiliation scores: a gnarled trunk of a tree flays my insides. The lurid wet sounds as he plunges two fingers in and out make my face and neck even hotter. I'm on fire as his hand runs down my arm, chasing goosebumps away with his scalding touch.

He curls his fingers inside me, grazing over my g spot, his hand on my shoulder moves to my breast, squeezing and kneading, pulling and tugging on my nipple. He bends his neck, and he bites at the space between my neck and shoulder hard enough to bleed. Gasping, I rise on my toes, and I don't know if it's to get away or give him more room.

"Get on your knees," he orders, his voice pushes out as if from a long distance.

Is this what being weak in the knees feels like? He orders me to get on my knees, I might fall to them. The only thing holding me up are his hands. The one with two fingers inside me making lewd sounds and the other massaging my breast. He's turning me into a cock slut for him, whoever he is.

"C-C-Conor?" My breath stalls in my throat as my orgasm starts racing to the finish line, and he removes himself from inside me. A sob drops from my chest as frustration and a deep emptiness fills the space where his fingers had just been.

"Conor who?" His voice leaks danger and ominous possibilities to come. "Do what I said, cock slut. Get. Down. On your. Knees. Now."

His hard hand reaches down, grabbing my hair, pulling down until I feel he's going to yank it out of my head unless I do what he wants. Slowly, I lower myself to my knees, joints snap to my added embarrassment.

"Open my pants and take my dick out." I quiver at his powerful, demanding voice, so deep they're almost a whisper; my hands shake so hard it takes me a few times to do what he wants, the button and zipper just out of reach every time I try. He doesn't say anything, doesn't downgrade my abilities to make fun of me. I stop what I'm doing while he waits patiently as I fist my hands, willing the control I need over my fear. I can do this. I know it's Conor. Those eyes. I know it is. I want to please him, pleasure him. Give him everything I have in me.

I didn't get a good look at it before when we had sex a couple days ago, but it's right in my face now. I didn't realize the tip was pierced. I don't know what this piercing is called, I don't want to hurt him at all.

"Hands behind your back, mouth open, tongue out." These are instructions I'm used to. He still has a tight grip on my hair; he releases me and grabs closer to my scalp for a better hold. "Do it."

I move my hands to my back, resting them at the spot above my ass, open my mouth wide, and stick my tongue out. Staying like that, waiting for his next command.

He doesn't move, stands still, black demon eyes staring down at me, the hideous white face frozen and lifeless. I wait like the good girl I am for an order or instruction. I move my thighs imperceptibly, the tingling and itching more than I can take.

"I didn't say you could move. You are such a needy cock whore, aren't you." This is not a question but a fact I know.

I freeze, waiting as he leaves me, hands behind my back, mouth open, tongue out. Waiting. It's such torture.

Without warning, he grabs my face in his other hand and forces his dick deep inside my mouth, all the way to the back, choking me.

CHAPTER SIXTEEN

Conor

I yank her head back enough so I can force my dick down to the back of her throat, holding myself there, my own head back as her throat strangles my cock in her tight depths.

Her throat is pure heaven, and when she swallows? Fuck, I'm about to nut now. I fucked up when I lifted my mask high enough to bite her and then lowered fast. Luckily, her eyes were closed. She knows it's me, but she's still not sure this is what takes this game to the next level. I have to hurry because I'm not sure how much more time we have left, and I want her face down in the dirt when I fuck her again.

Savvy is the perfect submissive, at least Dave did that, but he didn't do it the right way. Not by beatings and criticizing but by love and praise.

I shove my cock harder down her throat until her mouth presses against the base, her throat bulges, tears and snot run down her face. I wrap my hand around the front of her throat, feeling the bulge of my dick deep in her throat. It's the most beautiful sight I've ever seen.

Thrusting harder but not hard enough to hurt her, only to show my dominance, I have an overwhelming urge to pull my mask off and kiss her. Kiss her tears away, it will halt our fun. This game is everything.

My balls tighten, and I can feel myself ready to come. I don't want to, but I can't hold back. I come down her throat, and she gags as I flow down her throat in one long burst. She reaches out, clutching at my thighs as she can't breathe, and I release her hair, grabbing her throat instead. I won't hurt her, but I will take her to the edges, showing her her limits. How far she can go.

I move out of her mouth, and she bends over, her body shakes as she coughs, her face almost touching the ground. I give my watch a quick glance. We have an hour left. Plenty of time.

Savvy lifts the edge of her silk tank top, wiping her face, and looks back up at me, her eyelids heavy, filling with her lust. She loves what I do to her, she's probably soaking wet. Hmm, what should I use? Pussy or ass. I'm sure she's had a cock in both at some point. I don't know how long it's been, so her ass could be pretty tight. I shudder thinking about her ass strangling me.

"Come. Turn over." My demands are forceful but not mean. She's been trained to obey, so my tone will force her to do whatever I instruct. She's the perfect plaything. She is more, I just haven't discovered how more.

"How long has it been since someone has been in your ass?" Her green eyes widen, and she takes a step back. I grab her arm so she can't go any further. I shake her arm. "How long?"

"Years. Dave said." She lowers her head and blushes. "He said I was too tight and too much trouble. He only did it the one time."

I shake my head at how stupid Dave is, how irrevocably stupid he is. He's wasted such a gem all these years. "Yeah, that will be a no go now, then. Another time.

"Hands and knees. I will not repeat myself a third time. If I do, there will be consequences you won't like." I let her go, waiting to see what she's going to do. It takes her a minute. She gazes up at my neutral-faced mask and decides I mean it, turning her back and lowering herself slowly to the ground. I lay my hand between her shoulder blades and push her chest into the dirt, her shorts-covered ass waiting for me.

That ass of hers, I'd like to tear her shorts off, but she'll need something to wear back to the house. So I pull the elastic waistband out and pull them to her knees, letting them puddle in the dirt.

Seeing her naked ass makes me want to bite it, leaving my mark, I don't want the chance of her seeing my face. It will ruin the game. I let her leave her tank top on, it's loose enough I can work with it.

"Don't look back," I order.

I run my hands over her rear, pinching and molding her luscious flesh. Staying here and worshiping her flesh for hours is tempting, a temptation I can't give in to.

Parting her cheeks, she's starting to drip, she's so excited for this game we are doing. I insert three fingers inside her, she grunts at the initial intrusion. She starts pushing back as I move my fingers in and out, she's ready. I'm not quite yet.

I yank my fingers out, not being able to take the want anymore. I plunge my dick inside her, my mouth slackens at how tight and blissful being inside her is. She moans, her body shuddering and acting like a wild woman on crack. I wrap my fingers around her throat, pulling her back more, her moan strangles as she pushes her ass against me. I take off running, pushing in and out of her faster and harder, sweat pouring off my face under the mask. I slap my hand against her ass, the way she jiggles every time I slap a cheek, groans throttle through my throat at breakneck speed.

Not sure how much longer I can last, my orgasms have never been this short before, but she's perfection. Savvy is my perfect sexual match. The slap of flesh against flesh, the lurid picture of our fluids mixing is a graphic and vulgar sound with her cheeks spread wide and my cock humping in and out her pink pussy. She screams as I shove into her again. I slap my hand over her mouth, my fingertips digging into her cheeks. With my hand covering her mouth and her face pushed into the dirt, she can't scream anymore. Normally, I wouldn't care, but if one of the guards gets back early and hears her, they might get concerned and try to help her. As if she wasn't enjoying herself.

Raw, unadulterated lust surges through me as she tries to reach back and touch me. I lean forward, running my mask down the side of her face and over her back as if mine were touching her. Keeping this game up is hard when all I want to do is kiss and bite at her, showing everyone she is mine.

I fuck into her harder, my balls tighten until I can't stand it anymore, flooding her cunt with my cum. She jerks, her body tightening, and the only thing holding her up is my arm. I remove my hand from her mouth, turning her face roughly to look at me, stuffing my thumb in her mouth for her to suck. Tears run down her face, not in fear or anger, it's in...in. She wants more. Her mouth slackens even as she runs her tongue up and down and rolls around, her head thrown back as my arm is around her waist now. She gives one long, drawn-out moan and falls limp in my arms, her eyes mostly closed.

I'd better hurry back with her, I don't want any of the guards to see her covered in my cum, this mask on my face. They might get the wrong idea. Fuck. I look down at the woman limp in my arms. There is only one outcome now to this story. "Savannah, you are mine."

CHAPTER SEVENTEEN

Savannah

I stretch out in bed, pain spurts in different areas of my body. I moan, one hand goes to the left side of my neck, which feels extra sore. And my butt, the pain there is just as bad.

The room I'm in is dark except for a light coming from the bathroom. I turn my head in the other direction and find another small light there. I can't remember what day it is, obviously it's night now.

Slowly, it starts coming back to me. What happened early this morning in flashes. Conor coming home. Me trying to hit him, thinking it was Dave. Conor calling me little mouse and telling me to run, and everything after that comes roaring back like a hurricane.

My stomach clenches and my heart drops and rises like a rocket remembering everything after. It was thrilling and desperate at the same time.

I sit up, and my hands toss my mess of hair away from my face. Something tickles my cheek; I rub my fingers through the area and a leaf comes into my hand. I must be filthy. I throw the comforter away from my body and see I'm still dressed in the clothes from this morning. Now covered in dirt, smudged leaves, and cum. Both his and mine.

My stomach churns in hunger, I can't remember the last time I ate, probably yesterday some time. I can't go down looking like this. Shower and fresh clothes first.

As I walk around the end of the bed, I pull the comforter and sheets off and drop them on the floor to get later. A few more steps, and I'm in the attached bathroom and decide a bath will help with my bruises and pain. I turn the water on hot and step to the double sinks, picking my brush up and getting all the dirt, twigs, and leaves out before I wash it.

A half hour later, I'm still in the tub, feeling better with the hot water and Epsom salts I found in the cabinets. I also found some lavender bath salts. I wonder what woman stayed here with him. This feeling I have about another woman living here is something I've never felt before. I lean my head back, water drips from my hair, running down my face, mixing with sweat from the heat of the water temperature I add occasionally.

I consider and evaluate the feeling in my chest. My heart is a dead weight with little beats making me sad. Why am I sad? I've only really known this guy a few days, I never really knew Conor before.

Raising my hands to my cheeks, I swipe at the wetness. Am I crying? The heavy burning I feel in my head makes me feel I am. Why am I crying? He means nothing to me other than a guy keeping me safe. For now. What about later? How long will I be a prisoner here from my husband? Until he decides to divorce me?

I mean, I must only be a plaything for Conor, I can't be anything for him. I have nothing to give him other than sex. I'm sure he has housekeepers here, so doesn't need me for that. I need to make my own money. I have no education other than a high school diploma; I married that rat bastard right out of high school.

No education. No career chance. No idea of how to be on my own. I've always been taken care of and told what to do. That's why I feel so sad. The tears drift down my face, dripping to mix with the bath water. I'm useless to anyone.

I can't move in with my mother, my father is dead, but as far as I know, she's still alive. I heave a huge sigh; she'd want me to stay with Dave. I haven't seen her in...fifteen years? Dave took everyone away from me. That son of a bitch isolated me from everyone in my life and his.

Now I'm getting mad, and that's making me cry harder. I've never been one to feel sorry for myself, even when I'd been beaten and kept in a cage. I'd been scared I'd be forgotten about and die there. Feeling sorry for myself will never get me anywhere. I have to take care of me.

Now.

I decide to get out of the tub before I'm a total all-over prune and scramble ungracefully when the door opens. Water sloughs off my body, and I try to hide my breasts and private area from Conor's view. He strides over, standing over me, removing my arm from hiding my breasts. He takes one in his hand, his thumb flicks over the nipple; my heart leaps and races to an end I anticipate.

"Hiding what's mine?" He smirks, seeing what he's doing to me, pleased with the way my breaths lacerate my throat. "Aren't you?"

I try to breathe, but every breath sticks in my throat. I force a deep breath. "I belong to no one. I went through that already. I'm mine."

He smiles, all teeth, and the hand that had been playing with me tucks two fingers under my chin. "Little mouse, you might not know it yet. I'm not here to subjugate you against your will. I'm here to bring yourself out. Make you realize what a queen you are and can do anything you want. What do you want to achieve?"

That question hits me like a blow across my chest. Achieve? "I...I don't know. I've never had a choice."

"Now you do. What did you want to do in high school?" He takes a step closer, the only thing separating us is the edge of the tub. His t-shirt is getting wet, and I'm sure he can feel my hard nipples.

"I...I can't remember. It was so long ago." It's hard to get the words out, hard to think.

He leans closer and touches his lips gently to mine for one stolen breath. And another.

Conor pulls barely away, his lips still barely not touching mine. "Now you can." He turns and walks away, my body throbs with a craving at the way his wet shirt clung to the front of his body, the bumps and grooves of his chest and abdomen makes my clit pulse with the heat from my blood. I start to sink back into the now cooling water.

"Don't touch yourself or there will be consequences." His voice streams through the air, fast and furious.

Leaving me alone with an inextinguishable fire deep inside, building to a wildfire, ready to explode to a firestorm.

CHAPTER EIGHTEEN

Conor

The hardest thing I think I have ever done is walk away from her. I know she's wanting and needy by the way she caught her breath and how red her face is. I've made it harder for her by telling her she can't pleasure herself in place of me.

Savannah needs to know who she is now. She needs to become her own person and decide what she wants to do with the rest of her life. I want her by my side as my future wife, but what I want isn't important. What she wants is.

My phone rings, and I see it's Reel. I'm tired of this shit. He better have found him.

"Yeah."

"Got him," Reel crows, the excitement in his voice makes him shout.

I walk to the end of the hallway, shooting one quick glance in the direction of my room, walking down the stairs. "Where is Charlie?"

"You're not going believe this. He's in L.A."

I hold the phone away from my face and stare at it, disbelief in my tone. "I thought he was in Vegas."

"He was a few days ago. Now he's in L.A. You're not going to believe where." He's crowing through the phone. "At the Four Seasons!"

"What?" The Four Seasons, one of the more expensive hotels in Los Angeles. How can he afford that?

"I know, huh. I couldn't believe it either. How can he afford that?"

Once I reach the bottom of the staircase, I pace back and forth in front of it, my mind on Savannah and that fucker Charlie Norton. My thoughts zero in on Savannah and the way she looked a few minutes ago. Naked, her hair wet, with beads of water drying on her skin, looking like a siren of the sea. All she needs to do is open her mouth and sing me a song of destruction to make me follow her to my death.

"Look, Conor. I'm going to work on him a day or two. See what he's going for. That fucker must be working on something big, maybe one of the mafias. I'll look into it and you chill, look after that girl." His voice is a smug asshole.

"How did you- Never mind." I shake my head. He's a master of the dark web.

"I know everything," he says in a deep tone a psychic would use and laughs; he pretends to be an evil Joker. If I could see his face, it would probably be painted with that demented, red grin.

"Yeah, never mind. Okay, call me when you find something out."

"Over and out, mon capitaine." I open my mouth to respond, but an immediate click lets me know he's gone.

I shake my head, biting my upper lip and walk to the kitchen, my head down as I think. The only thought I can see still is Savannah. I need to stop thinking of her naked, but it's hard. Really hard, and I am.

I know she must be hungry; she never ate this morning and fell asleep in my arms as I carried her back to the house just before the guards arrived. I stand at the refrigerator, trying to decide what to make for her, and decide fuck it. Pizza sounds perfect.

"Conor?" I jerk my body around and almost plow into her, concentrating on what to eat. Like it is the answer to the world's problems.

"Pizza."

"What?" She looks so confused I want to laugh, but I've learned when I was married, not a good idea with a woman.

"I'm going to order pizza. I don't think you've eaten today at all. What do you like on it?"

"Um. Vegetables. Cheese. I haven't had it in years." She brushes her damp hair away from her face.

"Why not?" I'm shocked at what she told me. It's not as if Dave was broke and couldn't afford it.

"Well, um." Her voice drops to a whisper as if hoping I won't hear. "Dave thinks I'm too fat, and I'll just gain more weight."

My shock has turned to outrage for her. How can he say that? She's a goddess with curves a man can spend forever mapping.

"Well, you don't have to worry about that anymore. You can eat what you want. So, it'll be pizza tonight." Her life will change even more now. She's going to learn about being the woman she wants to become.

THE NEXT MORNING

After dinner last night, we watched a scary movie she'd never seen on the sofa, and she fell asleep. I carried her up, and I slept in one of the other rooms. I was afraid I'd give in to the temptation that is Savannah Collier.

We had a nice breakfast where I made her pancakes with strawberry syrup, and now, we're clothes shopping.

We've gone in and out of the high-end designer stores in Bay City while she complains about the cost. Cute. I can afford anything I want from the money from my great grandfather's inheritance handed down to me, I don't need to work, and I want to make a difference. I need the opportunities from my job with the department for me to find these released criminals. But with Reel, I'm using the department's resources less and less all the time. Soon, I might have to quit so I can spend more time on what I want to do.

She still hasn't bought anything, and I might have to for her. She needs more clothes; she hasn't brought enough with her, if she won't pick anything out, I will for her.

I watch every time she touches something and checks the price. I motion with one finger to an attendant. She hurries over, I lean closer. "Note what she looks at and pick a color that will suit her. Make a pile."

She nods and walks a few steps away, watching what Savannah looks at.

I stroll over to some sexy lingerie, searching through them, and find some things I think she'll like. Even if she doesn't, I know I will. I pull out a red number, a red thong attached to a lacy red nightgown-type that comes only to the top of her thighs. It's split up the sides. I also pick up a light blue silk teddy, open at the crotch and ass. I think I'll have her wear these tonight.

A male voice catches my attention, sounding familiar. Savannah says, "No." And that really catches my attention.

I swivel, Dave looms over Savannah, terror on her face and a wide grin on his. Her shoulders are slightly hunched, her green eyes dark with her fear, a toothy smile showing her teeth, a prey animal barring it's teeth in submission to the much larger predator. That's fucking it. I toss the lingerie to the floor and storm over, berating myself for not watching closer. It's my fault he's tormenting her now.

CHAPTER NINETEEN

Savannah

"Here you are, wifey." The voice I hate more than anything says behind me. I spin, my heart locks in my throat, the key tossed and lost at him here. Dave has a huge grin on his face, the one that has always promised beatings to come. The bright, open, friendly feeling of the clothes shop is now shrouded in a corrupt, vile feeling I can taste. Oily and black like a fiend from hell. A diabolical camouflage of his true nature. I hunch my shoulders down, ready for the strike.

He grabs my forearm; his hand tightens into a fist, crushing my wrist between his fingers. I cry out, "No."

"You're coming back with..."

A large hand grabs him by the shoulder, tossing him away, but I'm still attached to Dave. I go flying behind them, still held by the wrist as Conor hits Dave on the jaw. Dave releases my arm as he falls backwards, landing hard on the tile floor with a loud thud. I stumble forward, waving my arms around, trying to catch my balance.

Conor stands in front of me protectively, his hands at his sides loose and ready to strike again. "No, she's not."

"She's my wife," Dave sneers, getting up from the floor, blood leaking from a split on his lip, a bruise already forming on his jaw.

"And she's ready for the divorce papers. Think I'll contact my lawyer and have him send them to you," Conor counterattacks, his fists on his hips, looming over a slightly shorter Dave. He's ready to do whatever it takes to protect me, but does he really have feelings for me or is it a way to get more from me. Is he even more depraved than Dave?

"No, I won't sign them. She's my wife. Has been for eighteen years and will be. Forever. Till death do us part. Right, Savannah?" He glares at me, the last word a threat of what he can do. His eyes dark with a promise of what he will do to me if he gets his hands on me again. I've embarrassed him. If I go back with him, death will be a relief.

"She'll never go back. I'll make sure she gets to live the life she wants and never had before. With you. You ruined hers. She might ruin yours now. Leave, Dave. I'm warning you." Conor takes a large step forward, his body right up against Dave's, threateningly. Daring him to respond.

Dave turns and looks innocently at the attendant. "You see him threatening me? I have witnesses." He smirks at Conor as if he has the upper hand.

The employee's panicking gaze leaps from one of us to the other. Finally, she says in a firm voice, "The three of you must leave or I'm calling the police."

Dave's shocked and arrogant voice thunders through the room, "Do you know who I am? I'm the next senator for California. You'd better watch yourself."

The woman looks uncertain for a moment, her eyes jump from the two men and then rallies, "You might be running for senator, but if I call the police and say you're threatening this woman, I think something different will happen to your end game. Don't you?" She raises an elegant, plucked eyebrow at him. Both Conor and I try not to laugh at my husband being put in his place for once.

He glares at all of us and backs toward the entrance to the store, blustering as he goes. "You'll all regret this. I'm an important man. Conor and Savannah, you both especially."

He turns and stomps to the door of the store, turning his head back. "Have you had her ass yet? Got it nice and loose for you." He smirks as my jaw drops and fire burns my face, turning back and out the store. Dave gets into a Porsche – new? – parked in the handicapped space, and drives off, speeding down the street and making an illegal U-turn and almost causing a three-car accident in his self-importance.

We look at each other, and I start to apologize. "I'm sorry. I'm sorry. I'm sorry he threatened you."

The employee walks over and pats my shoulder. "I'm glad you got away from that asshole and found a man to take care of you and protect you." She looks at Conor.

"If you need any help in reporting him, let me know. He needs to be taken down a lot of steps and put in his place."

This woman who is older, maybe in her fifties, her face unlined so it's hard to tell, but it's her attitude. Confident. Her dark hair in an elegant up-do, darker skin tone glowing, and is so sweet. After her initial fear of Dave, she stood her ground to take Dave out.

I reach out and wrap my arms around her shoulders. She's a couple inches taller than I am, but she understands, and we hug each other tight. As only new friends can. I haven't had one since Dave isolated me from everyone.

"Here's my card." She hands me a maroon business card with the name of the store on the front. She turns it over, and Doris Jensen is written on the back with a phone number. I assume it's hers. "Call me anytime. If you need help." She jerks her head in the direction Dave left. "Or you just want to talk. I like making new friends, dear."

I hold the card in between both my hands and hold it to my chest, excitement zips through my veins like hasn't in a long time. It's different from with Conor, this might be a special friendship I don't want to lose.

Conor reaches into his back pocket and pulls out his wallet, going through it. He pulls out a card and hands it to Doris. "This is my home number. If you want to talk to Savannah, just call here. She or I will call you back. Thank you for everything." He holds his hand out to her, and she takes it in hers, and they shake.

He smiles at her, turns, and grabs my hand. I just realize I'm shaking in reaction to all the drama that happened.

His hand strokes my back up and down, and he leans down, kissing the top of my head. "Shhh. It's okay, Savvy. He's gone now."

"But he's always going to come back. He'll never let me go," I sob, resignation deepens the sigh in my throat. Shaking my head, I cover my face with my hands. Defeat washes throughout my body, waves getting bigger and bigger until I feel I might drown in them.

"Didn't I tell you before I'll keep you safe?" Conor leans down, wrapping his hands around my face and kissing my lips with a sweetness I have never felt with a man before. It destroys my heart.

"Yes, but-" He doesn't let me finish.

"I fucked up, Savvy. I'm sorry. It will never happen again. He will never get to you again." The sorrow in his voice and face makes me believe he believes it, but Dave always gets what he wants. Pure evil always wins.

"Okay, Conor. I believe you." I want him to think I feel completely safe with him, but there will always be a tiny inkling in the back of my mind that Dave will be coming, and he won't be able to keep me from him.

"Let's go." He grabs my hand in his, pulling me along behind him. The employee stands with her hands to her mouth, her eyes shoot sparks of love as if she just watched a swoony rom-com movie, and he's the hero. Maybe in her eyes, she did. "Bag up all that stuff she was looking through and whatever you think she'd like and send them here." He nods to the card he gave her.

We leave without any bags and go to his car. The drive to his home is silent, both of us cloaked in our own thoughts and worries. I shoot him glances, not sure what his mood is. I know he promises to protect me, but men lie to get what they want. Right?

He's already gotten it, even in depraved ways, but he's never hurt me like Dave has. Conor's made sure I enjoyed myself as well. So, that makes him better than him. I hope so, I have to keep a sharp eye on him. I can't trust him yet, I thought I loved Dave at first, too, because, at first, he was good to me. I can't let my heart control me this time. I might not be able to escape from him. No one else will come to protect me.

I bite and pull my upper lip into my mouth as we pull into the long driveway, on pins and needles, waiting to see what will happen next. Unbuckling the strap across my body, I release my upper lip and go to open the door, but it opens for me. Conor holds his hand out for me, and for a second, I don't know what to do. No one has ever treated me like this before. Like someone to be protected and cherished. I don't know why I don't completely trust Conor like I should, he's only treated me good. I guess it's because that's what I've learned about men. I hope I learn something else from him. Only time will tell the truth.

Hesitant, I place my hand in his, letting him pull me out and into his arms. He holds me close, our bodies together, drawing our strength from each other. He releases me with a light kiss on my lips.

I'm ready to walk away with him, our hands together, when I hear a slight sound. I stop and listen again. Conor looks at me, a puzzled expression on his face. A meow. I hear it again. I walk over to some lavender plants, parting the leaves to search deep inside the plants. There it is, a gray and white kitten.

The poor thing is thin, dirty, and its eyes are plastered together with sickness. I don't know how it found its way inside through the bars with how sick it is.

"What are you doing with that?" Conor's lip is lifting with disgust at the poor baby.

"I'm going to take care of it." I turn back to his car and open the passenger door, looking at him behind me. "I need you to take us to a vet."

"What? I'm not doing that." He gazes with disgust at the limp body in my hand. It's so sick I'm not even sure it's still alive. The kitten opens its mouth, and a slight sigh escapes, the mouth staying open. I hope that doesn't mean she just died. I can't keep thinking it, so I'm saying she's a she.

"Please, Conor. I've never wanted anything more than a pet. Except to get away from Dave, but I need this now. Please." I plead to him with my eyes, putting everything I have into it. I want this more than anything.

"Okay. Okay. Look on my phone for a close vet. Hopefully they'll see it right away." His grumbles are more special than anything, and I jump into the SUV, putting the tiny thing in my lap and putting the shoulder harness on.

He grumbles all the way to his side, I can see his lips move, but I see a tiny, tiny smile he's hiding. He'll do whatever I want. The idea makes my heart do a little leap, and I take the phone he hands to me and look through Google to find the nearest vet.

An hour later, we go home empty-handed but with the assurance the boy kitten should be ready to leave in a couple days. I'm so excited, it'll give us time to get whatever a kitten needs. I'm starting to feel maybe I can have a normal life. This is what I've always wanted. I think now I might finally get it.

CHAPTER TWENTY

Conor

Two days later. I can't believe this, but I'm taking a kitten home. When I was a kid, I had a dog, but when he died ten years later, I swore I'd never have another pet. I couldn't handle the grief.

I will do whatever Savvy wants, though, even if it's doing what I don't want. I mean, it's nothing that will hurt her, so it's okay with me. The vet's office called before she woke up, and I decided to surprise her. We set up one of the spare bedrooms for Jason. What a name for a cat. For him to get used to everything and to get well. She researched the healthiest diet for him, and everything is waiting for the arrival of the little prince. He is cute.

Back home, I carry the crate we had bought online and into the next room over, his new designated home. I open the door to the crate and take him out, now clean and free of fleas. For an extra charge, the vet gave him a bath and made sure any fleas were dead. He's still too sick for flea medicine, and since I'm sure he will never set one foot outside, he'll never need it. Jason will live the good life now. I had put a tiny refrigerator in his room so Savvy won't have to go all the way downstairs twice a day to get his meds. I've tried to think of everything they might need.

I carry him into the bedroom and rest his body against a still sleeping Savvy, she's been sleeping a lot the past couple days. Must be all the stress she's been under.

Jason snuggles closer to Savvy, and I smile, wanting to see her reaction to him when she wakes up. I pick up the arm chair in the room and carefully set it down so I can watch them and see her reaction when she wakes up.

This is all I want for her. To make her happy. I know she doesn't completely trust me yet as a man. I know she wants to. She wants to love and be loved more than anything, there's that trust issue again. I can wait. I have forever to wait for her if I have to.

All I do is watch like the stalker I am. I barely blink. Jason opens one blue eye to stare at me, then close, it. He has eyes of two differing colors. Heterochromia. We didn't see this at first because his eyes were stuck closed, the vet says it's very rare. I know Savvy will adore him no matter what he looks like. I growl at the way he's snuggling up against her so close. I can't believe I'm jealous of a kitten. That's where I want to be, but my front over her, fucking her from behind. Soon I have to get a plug into her ass. I don't care what Dave insinuated, I don't believe he's fucked her in a long time, she told me he didn't, whether her cunt or her ass.

My eyes grow heavy watching over them, it's rare, I usually won't fall asleep if I'm on watch, but like her, things have been so crazy I haven't had much sleep.

A squeal makes my eyes snap open and makes me leap to my feet, reaching for a gun that isn't there.

"Thank you. Thank you. Thank you." Savvy has Jason in her arms or hand as he isn't much bigger. She runs the three steps over and smacks me on my cheek with her lips. "I've never been happier. Come on, Jason. Let's take you to your room and get you something to eat."

She skips out of the room, happier than I've ever seen her. She acts younger than she ever has. Her whole life has been doing what her parents and Dave told her to do, never what she wants. Now she gets that chance, and I'm glad I gave that to her. And also to see her in my old t-shirt that comes down mid thigh, when she bends over, I get to see the tiny thong I bought her. I threw out her granny panties, all she's allowed are the thongs or nothing. I haven't gotten her used to no panties yet, I'm giving her time. We haven't had sex since the forest, allowing her time to trust me as a man and not feel used.

SAVANNAH

Conor is being so good to me, how can I not trust him. He wouldn't go through these motions of making me happy, he'd only have to throw me in a room and have his way with me, not give me a kitten I want and pick him up from the vet and watch me sleep. No one has ever been so good to me, not even my parents. In the back of my mind, I still have this little thought of *what does he want in return?*

I take care of Jason. Make sure his litter is fresh and add some replacement milk to some canned food to make sure he gets enough calories. The vet thought he was too young for anything else.

I leave him growling at his food, I'm amazed with how well he's doing with how sick he was only a couple days ago, a soft bed close by, and go back to my room, which is now empty. The disappointment racing through me is upsetting. I shouldn't be disturbed by it. I'm used to disappointment, whether it's mine or someone telling me I'm the disappointment.

Leaving the old t-shirt on I love so much –- it's Conor's police academy one – I slip on a pair of black leggings over this thong he got me. I don't like the way it feels, wish I had my more comfortable underwear, but I think he threw those out. So, it's thongs or nothing, and I'm not comfortable with nothing.

My bare feet don't make a sound as I walk down the hallway and the two flights of stairs. The kitchen is right off the foyer, so I go there, thinking that's where he is, and I'm right.

He's at the counter making an omelet from the eggs and vegetables scattered around the counters. For a clean freak, he's a messy cook.

I stand at the open entry, watching him gather ingredients and mumbling to himself. It's so cute the way he wants to make sure I eat healthy meals. He also makes me decadent desserts, too.

"Omelets today?" I lean my shoulder against the door frame, my arms crossing over my chest. He jumps, not expecting me to be down so fast, I guess.

He shoots a quick glance in my direction before going back to the meal he's making.

"When do the house cleaners come? I haven't seen anyone yet. I can do some cleaning today." I hate not doing anything. I'm used to working from the time I get up until after Dave went to bed. I need to stop thinking of him, he's out of my life now.

He's frowning at me as he scoops the omelet onto a plate. "I don't need you to clean. They come in twice a week, and once a month they clean the whole house. I want you to relax right now. Order some books, take a class online, or do nothing. That's what I want from you." He cuts the omelet in two pieces, sliding half onto another plate and setting it in front of me. How do I make him understand? He picks his fork up, cutting into the eggs, and lifting it up to his mouth. His phone rings, and he sets the fork back down, glancing to see who was calling. "I've got to take this. Eat." He gets up, clicks on answer, and leaves me alone. "Yeah, hey, Reel. Whatcha got?"

CHAPTER TWENTY-ONE

Conor

"Yeah, hey, Reel." I'm glad he calls, being around Savvy and not fucking her is messing with me. I'm having a hard time reining in my dick. All he wants me to do is grab her, throw her to the floor, and fuck her till she screams my name. Or just screams her orgasm. "What do you have for me?"

"Hey. You're not going to believe this, but Charlie isn't far from where the other one was. Within a mile. Checking to see if they knew each other." I hear the clicks of the keys of his computer in the background. His fingers are moving so fast they're a blur of sound.

"Great. Check on it, and let me know. I'll make sure everything's ready in case tonight is a go." I hit end and continue up to my room to take a shower and get ready for the day. It's already getting late, noon, and I have a lot to do to get ready for tonight.

My foot is on the bottom step to the stairs when a soft, hesitant voice interrupts my thoughts, "Conor?"

I still, not turning to face her. I can't. She'll see how hard I am thinking about her and killing someone. I've become so fucked up. "Yeah?"

"Um. I've been thinking about what you said. You know about going to school? I thought maybe becoming a children's therapist? I've always wanted children, but Dave said it was my fault we hadn't had any yet. I'm defective."

I close my eyes and lean my head back as far as I can on my neck. Anger a burning fire in my chest. Can that man get anything right? Why would he say something like that to the wife you're supposed to love and cherish?

"I'm sorry. I know. Stupid idea, I don't know what I was thinking," she mumbles the words to me, and I turn around to see her start to leave, her head down.

"It's not a stupid idea, Savvy. I think it's a great idea, and if you want children, go to the doctor and see if it's true. If you can't, adopt. There are lots of children out there who would love to have a mother like you."

She turns back to me, a smile so bright it's blinding. "Really?"

"If you want to, pick somewhere local, so later you can go there or pick somewhere, wherever you'd like to live after Dave is taken care of, go for it." My voice is deeper than normal as I walk slowly toward her. I can't keep the desire out of my voice or body as my dick comes to full hardness. So hard the pain is consuming me.

"Yes." Her voice is a tiny mouse squeaking. She gazes up at me, her heart in her eyes, and all I want to do is cherish that heart for what it is. My salvation. She doesn't know it yet.

Our bodies are so tight against each other I know she can feel how hard I am. "If you don't want this, Savvy, let me know now. You won't get another chance again."

"Yes, Conor. I've been waiting."

I grab her hair by the back of her head, yanking her head back, and smash my mouth onto hers. Savvy clutches at my shoulders, moaning into my mouth, her leg wrapping around my ass. I lift her up, and both her legs are now around my waist.1 Without stopping, I stumble up the stairs to our room, the door a hard obstacle.

She settles that by reaching behind her back, struggling, and searching, finds the knob, and the door flies open.

I attempt to make it through the doorway, but with her in my arms and my lips on hers, it's difficult. It was hard enough getting us up here in one piece.

We're the perfect storm of clashing teeth, tangling tongues, grasping hands, our bodies begging to become one.

After bumping into the walls and bed posts a couple times, I lay her on the bed, staring down at her. Her green eyes dark with lust, legs spread and wanting.

I reach back, yanking my shirt off, almost tearing it in my impatience. The t-shirt I cared a lot about, I tear off her body, not caring about it anymore. Thank god she's not wearing a bra.

Her leggings, I yank down, her thong falls along with it. Now that she's finally naked, I kiss her again, this time more sweetly, once. Twice. Going down her body with tongue and teeth. Little nibbles here and there.

I make my way down her body, laving my tongue on her throat, nipping with my teeth, sucking her skin, and leaving as many hickeys as I can. I want everyone, including Dave, to see she's mine. I lift her breasts in my hands, sucking on her nipples, lightly biting at them.

Shoving her knees apart with mine, I move further down her body. "Do you trust me?"

She stares up at me, an unsure expression on her face. I run my fingers over her bare cunt, up and down, she's soaking wet for me, even if she doesn't want to admit she trusts me. I'll get her to admit it.

Her head falls back, staring at the ceiling, not wanting to admit her feelings with eye contact. If she looked me in the eyes, she can't avoid her feelings. I let this go for now, how she acts will tell me her true feelings until she can bring herself to admit to them. Maybe it's still too soon.

"Do you want to be my slut today?" I hook two fingers around her chin, lowering her head so she can look right into my eyes.

Hers are watery with unshed tears, starting to unfocus as she disassociates herself from me. I should have realized this would have been something Dave said to her. I have to remind her that it's me. Not him.

"Savvy. It's me. Conor. You want to be with me. Remember? I won't hurt you. This is all for you, your pleasure." I wait and watch her eyes, seeing her come back to me, before I plunge two fingers inside her, and her body jerks. I watch every twitch and twinge her face can have and add another finger, curling them inside her. Her body jerks harder, moving up and down, fucking herself on me This is what I'm looking for.

"Yes, Savvy. This is all for you. Take all your pleasure from me. Take all I can give you. Take it into you."

Her heavy pants fill the room, her body rocks with every plunge of my fingers inside her. Our rhythm gets more intense and physical, I don't know how much longer I can hold on without coming.

Her body stiffens, her cunt clamps down on my fingers, her mouth open in a silent scream, and she comes. Twitching and spasming, she finally goes limp in our bed. I lift my fingers, and her heavy-lidded eyes watch as I put them in my mouth, licking them clean. Yum.

CHAPTER TWENTY-TWO

Conor

My phone rings, and I slump my body onto the side of her. I can't believe my luck, at least if this is Reel, and I didn't get my release, she might realize this isn't all about me.

"Yeah."

"Conor, we've got him." His voice is high and shrill from his excitement. Reel lives for this kind of thing. He loves the hunt as much as I do, but we hunt in different ways. I go in and get my hands dirty, and he hunts digitally. It all ends the same way, finding our prey and tearing them to pieces.

I get off the bed, not wanting to disturb Savvy or bother her with what I do in my spare time. I leave the room, not wanting her to hear our conversation and our plans. I don't want her involved in any way in case this goes wrong somehow.

Going downstairs, I walk into my office and close and lock the door. This room was made soundproof when I inherited the property. You never know who's listening.

"Okay, Reel. I'm back. What have you got for me?"

"He's in cahoots now with the same cartel. They are helping him, and he's hiding not far from the other. I have the address, so whenever you're ready." He's hurrying in his eagerness. He's never told me why he's so into this and wants the bad guys permanently put away. I assume someone was hurt by a criminal. I've never asked just like he's never asked me. It's no one's business but our own.

"Tonight, we'll do this. I'll rest today, and about six, we can go over how we are handling this with the information you've gotten. Kay?"

"Yup. Talk later. Get some sleep. Wink, wink, and something to eat. It might be a long night." He clicks off, sometimes he's talkative and sometimes, like now, he's totally immersed in his target.

I sit in my large, upholstered chair behind my desk and lean my head back against the headrest. Unbelting my jeans, I unzip them and fist my hard dick, wanting to relieve my hurting balls. I'm sure Savvy is asleep now, and I don't want to wake her.

I don't have any briefs on, deciding commando was the way to go this morning, and I'm glad I did, I can take care of myself easier. I stroke myself, pulling and tugging hard on my dick, liking a touch of pain myself.

Savvy is stretching out on the bed in my imagination, naked, her hands on her own breasts, pulling on her nipples.

SAVANNAH

Conor has been gone for a while now. I throw a robe on, walking down the stairs to try and find him. It takes some time, but I've searched through the kitchen and all the bottom floor rooms except for one locked door. I lean my head against it to see if I can hear anything inside. I can't.

I decide to knock, and after a few minutes, and I decide to leave and turn away but the door opens. He looks uncomfortable standing in the doorway, his arms over his head against the top of the doorway and staring at me.

"Um, I got worried. Are you okay? You never came back." I have another one of his t-shirts on and leggings, I like them better than the expensive clothes he bought me. I've never worn anything like those, I've always worn jeans or leggings.

"Fine. Fine. Just getting some work done." He shifts his long, thick legs, and I notice his thick cock along his leg. That must be excruciating. Do I have enough guts to take care of that for him? I haven't had sex with Dave in at least two years, if not longer. I lost track because I was happy about it, now, I'm not. I got a taste of good sex and want more. I understand the concept of being a sex addict, that's all I think about now, when we are going to do it next.

I raise my head and walk toward him, waiting for him to move aside. My heart is in my throat, suffocating my breaths, feeling like there's a bag over my head, no oxygen for me to breathe, waiting to see if he will move aside so I can go in.

He takes his hands away from the frame and steps aside, I close and lock the door with a loud click.

"What are you doing, Savvy?" Conor cocks his head to the side, studying my reaction.

I try to appear calm and not the crazy person I feel inside. I walk toward him, and he backs away until he's up against the desk. He gives a slight laugh, "Savvy, what are you doing?"

My body walks between his legs, parting them so I can fit my body between them. I kneel, reaching for his belt, still not saying a word.

"Wait. Wait. What are you doing? Do you want to do this?" His pants are loud and hectic in the otherwise silent room.

"Yes, I want to give you pleasure, too. I can see you are in pain. I don't like that." The tongue of his belt flaps loose, and I reach out, unzipping his jeans slowly. I want to stretch this out for as long as I can. Prolonging the anticipation.

I stretch my tongue out, licking along my bottom lip, wishing he was already in my mouth so I can taste him. I hope I can do this good for him.

He's not wearing any kind of boxers or briefs, and his cock springs out, standing wide and strong, weeping at the tip in frustration. I smooth the fluid along his cock, grabbing the base with both hands, moving up and down his length with one hand. I squeeze, and he groans, I glance up quickly to his face to see if I'm hurting him.

His head is down, watching, his eyes deeply hooded, bottom lip clenching between his teeth.

I must be doing it right because he gives me a tight nod, and I lean forward, taking him into my mouth.

"Hands behind your back." His voice is so deep and low it's almost a whisper. I love it when he talks like this, tingles zip through my body, and my breath locks in my throat every time he orders me to do something.

I do what he says, leaning my body forward to take more of him in my mouth, he juts his hips, forcing more into me. He does it again, grabbing my head on both sides of my skull to hold me in place. He forces more of his length and hits the back of my throat, and I gag, trying to get away, but with the hold he has on my head, I can't.

"Is your cunt wet? I want you to reach down and check. I bet it is."

I reach down and slip one hand into my leggings and under the thong I'm wearing. My finger slides through the gushing wetness at his ordering me and him forcing me.

"Are you? Show me."

I remove my hand, my face hot with embarrassment as I hold my hand out to him, his cock still in my mouth and hitting the back of my throat, tears dripping down my face.

He pulls me up by my wrist, his cock popping out and shoves my fingers into his mouth, humming in approval at my taste. My face heats to a firestorm at his appreciation. I've never had a man savor me like he is.

Conor removes my fingers from his mouth, thrusting inside mine again, grunting, "Don't come until I do."

The power he wears like a thick coat washes over me, erupting like a volcano, sizzling over my skin. This is something I've never felt before. Powerful. Giving him his pleasure gives his power over to me. I cradle it like the precious gift it is.

He groans again, this time long and hard, and his tip hits the back of my throat and down my esophagus. I struggle to breathe through my nose, drool drips from the corners of my mouth.

"I'm going to come. Don't swallow yet," he growls in a breath. His hand holds me by the back of my head in place, his cum floods my mouth, some leaks down my throat and out the sides of my lips.

"Open your mouth and let me see." I whimper but do as he says, opening my mouth so he can see I haven't swallowed yet. "You're my good girl, right?"

I nod up and down, still trying to hold his cum in my mouth at the same time.

"Go ahead. Swallow."

I do, it's like an ice cream sundae. Rich and creamy.

"Show me."

I open my mouth and show him nothing's there.

"Good girl." And I'm shocked at how that makes me feel.

CHAPTER TWENTY-THREE

Conor

I'm sitting a few houses away from where Charlie is living, in a nice home on Wilshire. It's a nice middle-class home. Not like the other guy. Of course, Charlie's not here, and I have to sit here and wait till he gets back.

He better not take all night; I have better things to do tonight. Like fuck Savvy until she passes out. Watching her earlier with my dick down her throat, drool dripping out of her mouth, was the highlight of the past couple of days. I need more of that. Much, much more.

I lean my head back against the headrest, tired of this waiting, when out of the corner of my eyes, I see a nondescript, older, gray Honda pull into the driveway. A man with a blue baseball cap on backwards gets out of the car, going to the trunk and opening it. I sit up straighter as he fiddles around back there and then lifts something wrapped in blankets and tied with rope. He carries it on one shoulder, bouncing it to get a better grip. As I squint to get a better look in the nighttime darkness, I see three fingers peeking out from one corner.

I press the contact in my Range Rover and call Reel. He picks up right away. "Yeah, whatcha got?"

"I think he's got one."

"One what?"

"A girl. He went into his trunk and got something big out, wrapped in a big blanket or comforter. I saw fingers, Reel. Fingers." I'm already grabbing my mask, my gun, and knife out of my murder bag, slipping it into the side of one combat boot. I grab two more knives, place one in my other boot, and the third in the holder attached to my belt.

My mask in hand, I add a device to disguise my voice to the mask, this time. I don't want to take any chances on being recognized in any way.

"Okay, I'm on it. He has one camera out by the front door. I have it off and there aren't any in the house. I wish there was someone else there to help you in this. I don't like you being alone doing this."

"Reel, I can't trust anyone else in this." I talk quietly, I have the car speaker on low, but I still look around for anyone. Can't take any chances.

"Yeah, I know. Put your phone on so I can hear everything going on and help direct you if needed."

"Yeah. Good idea. Okay, done. You'll be able to hear everything once I switch from car speaker to phone speaker." I open the car door and slide out along with the murder bag and put the gun behind my back under my jeans.

I lock the door, cross the sidewalk, and head over to bushes hiding the house from the street. How convenient for me. I walk up the driveway as if I belong, sliding on the mask and pulling my hoodie over my head. I try the doorknob and the door opens. Idiot, what does he think, no one will come in?

Quietly, I close the door, locking it behind me in case someone else decides to come in. I hear voices and follow the sounds, glancing around the interior as I inspect the place, in case someone else is in on this, whatever this is. I have my own idea, but I want to be sure before I slit his throat.

Nothing unusual as far as I can tell. He has a big screen TV in a smallish living room. Kitchen has dishes piled in the sink, pizza boxes piled in the trash, and beer bottles and cans everywhere. Typical lazy ass man leaving trash around if there's no woman to clean up after him. Entitled men like him disgust me. Well, after he's dead, someone else can take care of this.

I make my way to what looks like a door to a basement. Most houses in L.A. don't have basements, so it's interesting to me why this one does. I leave the door where it is, partially open. I drift around it, not making a sound in my boots, placing each one carefully on each step down.

Slipping my gun out from behind my back and a blade from my left boot, I try to peer around a sharp corner in the house. I think I see what might be steel bars, but I'm not sure. I need to get closer.

"Yeah, I've got another one. This one is young and fresh. Fresh meat. Not sure, but I think virgin. Yeah, you never know these days. Uh huh. Yeah. Bring cash and lots of it. I'm not selling this one cheap. Yeah, you can have a two-for-one. I'll give you one of the older bitches for free. Got too many here anyway. Yeah, get here soon. Okay. Bye."

"Here. Get her unwrapped and clean her up. Use that water over there, I don't fuckin' care where you get it the fuck from just clean her up." There's a slap and a sob, then nothing. I'm afraid he's going to leave, and I'm on the stairs. I look over the side and decide to jump, hoping my boots don't make too much noise when I hear another slap and a gurgle. I'm afraid to look and see what's going on, but I have to know if I'm going to get these women out of here safely. I finish making my way down the stairs and by the groans and gurgles, I know what's going on, and I'm beyond filled with revulsion. I slide a part of my mask out to see around the corner, and he's doing what I thought. He has a woman on her knees, his dick in her mouth. Forcing her, by the way he has his hand tightens around her throat, cutting off her air and his other hand on the top of her head as he skull fucks her. Her eyes are wide, the whites so prominent from here, searching for any way to escape. She wheezes as he slaps his pubic bone into her lips, drool dribbles out her mouth, splashing on her naked tits every time he pounds into her.

Fury cascades throughout my veins, a red-hot magma waiting to erupt. Her eyes half-close as she becomes weaker and weaker, his strangling fist doing the job he intended. Savvy and I did this same thing a few hours ago, the difference is it was consensual.

I raise my gun and take aim. She sees me, and her eyes widen again, and I fire at the back of his head. Blood and brain matter splatters around and on her, her face and naked body is covered in dark red and thick lumps. None of it bothers her.

"What the fuck, dude?" Reel shouts in my ear.

"I had to. He was strangling a woman. I know you can't see. You heard he's planning on selling a young girl, right?"

"Yeah, I heard. I understand why you did it, but, man...you've got to get out of there before they come. You don't know how many there are or how they're armed. Go, dude."

"I will, I just have to make sure they are okay."

"C-dude, go, you don't have time."

He almost gave me away in his upset. This mistake can't happen again. "Are you okay?" I say, turning my head to gaze right at her, my voice softer. I'm surprised the body fluids covering her aren't making her freak out. There's no way anyone will know who I am, even if they meet me again, with the voice modulator I'm using.

"Yes, yes. I will get us out of here. Now. Hurry, go. Thank you, señor." She has an accent, and with her using that last word, I know she's of Spanish descent.

I wave at her and turn, leaving the way I came, unlocking the door and leaving it open for them. I hope they get out in time, but with the discharge of my gun, I can't take any more chances. I grab my bag and race to my car, my head down so no one looking out a window can see my face, throwing the bag in the back and leaping inside, starting the car and driving off.

"Everything good, Reel?" I hope he knows what I mean about cameras along my roundabout way home. I tug my hoodie down and mask off, tossing it into the back seat alongside my murder bag. That thing is the only reason I could ever go to prison for what I do. I never leave witnesses who can ID me. I never even saw the young girl except for when he was carrying her. That woman is the only witness. All she sees is a devil.

A harbinger of death to wrongdoers.

CHAPTER TWENTY-FOUR

Savannah

I don't know what Conor does when he leaves here. Is he married with a wife and kids he has somewhere else? A second life?

I'm sitting staring out the living room windows, the lights surrounding the mansion bright in the darkness of the night. Alone for once, the guard in the room that monitors the cameras off for the night, and no one else has come to replace him yet. Not sure what that means, is Conor going to come and use me again? Is that his plan?

A shadow moves right outside of the light, I'm not sure if it's my imagination, I've been staring out for so long. I squint, trying to see if it's actually a person or nothing at all. My pulse spikes as another shadow shuffles, shifting the darkness, and I back up, my hand to my throat. It's not my imagination. I know someone or something is out there. It's got to be Conor playing mind games on me.

The gloom moves closer, the shadows coalescing into a human shape. Large, broad, threatening. "Conor, is that you?'

I get off the sofa, taking a step away from the window. And another. "Conor, this isn't funny."

The shadow forms into a body that rushes the floor-to-ceiling window brandishing a weapon, thrusting it, and glass shatters into the room. I turn to run, shrieking, but I'm grabbed by the back of my shirt and my hair in one grip, yanking me up to him.

He shoves a gun hard into my side, so hard I think it will at least leave a bad bruise if I come out of this alive. He moves his hand to my throat, cutting off my air. I claw at the hand, flipping my body, kicking out to hurt him so he'll let me go. My bare feet can't do anything, so I lift my knee up high, hoping I get him in his cock.

Of course, he anticipates my move and tilts his hips to the side and back, and my knee hits the inside of his thigh. He grunts at the hit and loosens his hold on my throat, but otherwise, doesn't acknowledge it.

He grabs my arms, shoving them behind my back and zip-tying them together. I've got to get away somehow.

"I was told to bring you back, but I can't fuck you. He'll never know. It's not as if the guy you're shacked up with doesn't fuck you. It'll be our little secret. Yeah?"

"Pl...please. No." I moan, he's a degenerate rapist, possibly murderer, and I don't know how to stop him. His face has acne scars and a long scar lengthwise down his face. Maybe from a knife. His clothes stink, I'm close enough to smell them.

"Awww. I know you want it, bitch. Beg me." His tongue licks up the side of my face, and I want to vomit. I close my throat, holding it back, but a sob escapes, not sure what he'll do to me if I throw up on him.

He yanks my head back further until it feels like my spine is going to crack. "You'll do what I say, cunt."

The sound of a door opening and closing makes us both jump. "Honey, I'm home."

It sounds like Riley, one of the outside guards. "Honey, are you there?"

I open my mouth to cry out, another sob escapes again, tears and snot run down my face, but a dirty hand slaps over my mouth. The wannabe rapist walks me in front of him, his other hand looped around my forearm. He walks me into the foyer where Riley stands, a big grin on his young face. But something's wrong, it doesn't look quite right. There's something going on I don't know about, but I'm the important piece.

CONOR

I knew something was wrong when I called to speak with Dan the cyber guy, and he didn't answer. I called Reel, then, and he immediately got into my cameras. I don't want to know how he had my codes.

I'm sitting at the gate, knowing something is wrong, and Reel shows me. The first camera he goes to is live feed in the living room, and Savvy is standing with a strange man holding her in his arms, one hand at her throat and the other in her hair. Reel adds the audio. I shouldn't be hearing this because now, all I want to do is commit murder. Bloody. Limb-cutting, violent murder. I'll start with his dick and balls.

"I was told to bring you back but not fuck you. He'll never know. It's not as if the guy you're shacked up with doesn't fuck you." He's more than dead. He'll be tortured first. "It'll be our little secret. Yeah?" he finishes, his tongue slides up her face, and she looks like she wants to vomit; instead, she sobs. "Awww. I know you want it, bitch. Beg me."

"Riley, I want you up at the house this second. I'm going around back. Pretend to be me," I grind each word out as if it's torture to say them, and it is.

"Boss?" He gazes at me, his eyes wide, not understanding what I'm telling him to do.

"We don't have time, Riley. We have to save her, and this is the only way. He's going to rape Savannah. Go. Now. Be me. Whatever you have to do to convince him and take his thoughts off her and anything else so I can sneak in." I leave the Range Rover, engine running, in park and race along the fence line along the trees. They are far enough away from the fence so no one can climb over if they don't mind dealing with the electrified barbed wire along the top. There are trees, though, lots of trees and bushes to give the property a forest-y vibe. That may be my downfall.

Every second wasted is more likely Savvy is getting raped. I need to hurry, and Riley had better be inside or he will be another I murder. Three in one night? A new high.

"Riley is inside. Pretending to be you, calling her *honey.* You better hurry. Riley isn't going to be able to hold out much longer." Reel's voice is quiet but intense, letting me know the situation is in crisis mode.

I run even faster, avoiding the windows, which there are a lot of. Too many. I might have to do something about that, I've become complacent in all the revenge plotting I've been doing.

I slide around the side of the mansion, almost sliding into the pool. Instead, I slip on gravel, making too much noise in the process. Hopefully, Riley has him distracted enough. I peek around the side of the broken window and mentally beat myself up again about my complacency. As soon as this guy is taken care of, that will be the next thing to do. Bulletproof windows.

He stands with his back to me, arguing with Riley, Savvy's back against his front. I stare at the broken glass, deciding the best way to climb through without giving myself away.

I carefully move the larger pieces and step through the open space, creeping toward him and Savvy. One hand holds a gun to the side of her head and the other, her bicep. I bite my bottom lip, concentrating on getting the best of him and still keeping him alive to get information from. And not getting Savvy killed. Top priority there.

I wish I could talk with Riley, but there's no way without the rapist knowing. I lurk closer, one step at a time, my pulse pounds loud enough I'm afraid he will hear. I meet Riley's eyes and give him a dip of my chin. I shove my gun at the back of his head where his skull meets his spine and hit him as hard as I can with the side of the gun, yanking him hard away from Savvy. Her body follows because of the hold he has on her. The gun explodes the bullet, but Riley has leaped forward and tilted her body enough the bullet slides past, entering the wall instead of her head.

CHAPTER TWENTY-FIVE

Savannah

The hand holding my arm tugs as he starts falling, and I go with him. I don't understand what's happening. Riley was standing in front of the stranger arguing with him, a big, fake grin on his face.

Hands grab me before I fall to the floor with the wannabe rapist. I turn my head to look behind me and see Conor. Of course, he came to save me. He always does now.

I don't know why I doubted. Conor has a knife, reaches out, and slices through the zip ties. I look up, and Riley has the man on the ground, on his front, his knee on the man's back, pushing him hard into the floor. The man is shaking his head as he's hauled up, Conor zip-ties his hands behind his back, blood flows from the wound on the back of his head. I'm surprised he's up and walking with how deep the wound looks on his shaved head.

The man's head is down, bobbing on his neck as Riley drags him out of the room and out of my sight. Conor reaches down and picks up a cell phone, putting it in the pocket of the hoodie he's wearing.

"Are you okay, Savvy?" He's leaning over me, looming, but it's not scary. It's welcoming, taking care of me. One arm around me, his hand cups my shoulder, concern for my well-being in every line of his body. This is why I, l-. No. I can't think that yet. I am not ready.

"I, I don't know yet. It just. It all happened so fast." I lay the side of my hand against my forehead, then run it down my face to wipe everything away. I'm a mess. My thoughts. My emotions. "I need. I need to go to the bathroom and clean up." I look around, half in a daze, not sure what just happened was real or a bad nightmare. It feels real. My face hurts, my whole body hurts.

He immediately lowers one arm and sweeps me into his arms like a bride, carrying me up the stairs to the bedroom. Our bedroom now. I try to protest him carrying me, but he doesn't listen.

Reaching his arm out, he opens the door and carries me to the bathroom, setting me on the counter. Conor reaches over, taking a washcloth, wetting it in warm water from the tap. He leans down, wiping my face as gently as he can, totally different from the man a few minutes ago.

The warmth from the cotton soothes me, his presence calms me as if I took a tranquilizer. I feel myself relax; tiredness immerses itself deep inside to my mental core. I've taken as much as I can today. My body starts slumping forward, and Conor holds me up with his other hand. I can let my mind release; he'll take care of me.

CONOR

I pull the covers back, laying her down in the middle of my bed. Yes, my bed. *Our bed*. Toeing off my shoes, I reach behind me, pulling off my shirt, and lay beside her. I gently tug her closer and lie her over me, her head on my chest over my heart. Her breaths are short and fast, making me think she's not sleeping deep. Her face, arms, and legs twitch in her mental distress.

I am slightly propped up by pillows and gaze down at her. I can't see her face, it's half-covered by her hair. I haven't been in a relationship since my wife was killed twenty years ago, so calming a woman is not something I remember. I think it's just instinct.

My hand rubs down her hair, catching a lock between my fingers, lifting it to my lips and running it back and forth over them.

A soft knock doesn't startle me, but it does irritate.

"Boss, I have news."

"Come." I'm not worried about him seeing Savvy, she's covered up to her neck.

The door only opens enough for his face to appear. "How is she?"

"Sleeping."

"The guy is waking up. What do you want to do?" His eyes and face are anxious, keeping his eyes away from Savvy.

"Keep him as uncomfortable as possible. I'll be down in a bit." I pull her even closer, ignoring the click as the door closes behind Riley, holding her cheek tighter to my bare chest. I thought I knew what love was when I married my wife all those years ago, but this is different. I don't know if it is love or obsession. I don't even know if there is a difference. All I know is I can't stand the thought of being away from her or anything happening to her. It would gut me. I spread my fingers wide, combing them through her hair, getting the tangles out. I've got to leave her now, I need to get business done by finding out who sent him. I have a more than strong idea, but I need proof.

I slip out from underneath her, regretting it instantly, there is nothing else I can do. This has to be taken care of now. Immediately. The longer this cockroach is still alive on this Earth, he will infect everyone with his deadly sickness. I'm doing this world a favor by getting rid of his foul stench.

Walking into the hall and down the stairs, I make my way to the usually locked door leading down to the special basement I had made. It is soundproof with special additions. The additions help with the screams and yells of pain and cries for help. I will take him apart piece by bloody piece.

The grunts I hear are the music to my soul I need for what I saw a couple hours ago. My heart rate kicks back up thinking about it. But I don't want my men to have all the fun, they need to leave me some of him.

My boots clomp on the steel steps I had put in for the auditory and mental torment imagery. "Hey, boys, leave me something to work with."

I step onto the concrete floor with drains set throughout the room. I walk over to the man they have tied with chains to a sturdy metal chair bolted to the floor. He's naked, his hands chained behind his back, behind the back of the chair, and each foot chained to a leg of the chair. He's not going anywhere unless we allow it.

His head hangs down on his neck, his eyes are swollen shut, blood drips in a steady stream from a corner of his mouth, and he has bruises covering his torso. Probable a few broken ribs at least.

I'm going to start with the friendly approach since the guys started the bad cop routine. "So, what's your name?"

My hands are in the front pockets of my jeans, and I slouch, pretending this isn't anything important. It takes a minute for him to slowly lift his head. He snarls at me, his bloody teeth have a few missing. They must be on the floor somewhere. I look down, searching. Aw, there's one.

I lift my arms and cross them over my chest, glaring at him, "Come one, I don't have all day. Or night."

"Fuck you." He spits a glob of blood at me, barely missing my boot. I glance down at the blob, oozing.

"Doing this the hard way, huh? I just want to find out who sent you, and we'll end your suffering right now. Kill you the easy way."

"Fuck you and the woman. He'll get her and fuck her up good." He sneers as if his questionable masculinity is not in question.

That has my anger flaring to that of a raging bull shown a red cape by a matador. Kill him slowly, it is, then.

"It's there, boss." Riley points to the black bag I use when I have a job. I didn't know Riley knew about what I was doing behind the scenes. This is worrying, but I can't worry about it now.

"Get everyone else out." I don't need any more witnesses.

Riley points to the door, and the other two men trudge out, looking over their shoulders. This is very worrying. Witnesses.

"Conor, I had to bring him in on this. You don't have to worry about Riley. I've thoroughly checked him out. He's good." Reel is always around, his voice echoes from the speaker on my phone in my pocket. Is he a real person or a figment of the internet like Max Headroom in the old TV series I used to watch when I was younger? How does he know how to appear, and how does he do that?

"Problems, detective?" The man laughs, and I narrow my eyes at him. "Everything not going your way? He said to fuck you up, and I have. How's the pretty lady doing? A little chunky for my taste, but her tits look good, even older like she is. I like 'em young, if ya know what I mean." He tries to wink at me, it's hard with his eyes swollen shut.

"Kill him. He knows nothing." I want to see if Riley will do what must be done. His eyes are wide, but his face is resolute and hard with his intention to do what he must do. Later, we'll have to talk about his future with me. I need more help. A second. He might be it.

He nods, taking a knife out from his belt. The man laughs even harder, laughing through the coughing and hacking from his broken ribs. He has a will of iron, I'll give him that. "He'll get her from you. He knows everyone important and will get her again. There's nothing you can do about it, he has enough money and influence."

I turn away to go back up to Savvy. I forgot about something, I've been too focused on her. "What about the missing men?"

Riley answers, "Knocked out. Three men. At least he didn't kill them."

I nod and start walking up the stairs. "Kill him and get rid of the body."

"No problem," Reel answers. "I know what to do and will walk him through it. Take care of your lady."

"Thanks, Reel. We need to discuss you tomorrow."

"I know. Something a long time coming." His amorphous voice is hard and yet soft, a fusion of the two.

CHAPTER TWENTY-SIX

Savannah

My eyes are so heavy I can't seem to open them. I'm so tired, I feel like I haven't slept in days. I know I'm lying in bed; it feels like I'm chained to it. I curl my fingers and hard flesh smoothes under my fingertips. My eyelids fly open, and I'm sleeping on Conor's naked body. The whole top of my body lies on his. It feels weird sleeping with a man, Dave never would, even when we were first married and in our honeymoon stage. Separate rooms.

He sleeps so deep he doesn't feel my body moving. I have an idea this is unusual for him; it makes me glad he can do this with me. Let himself go.

The comforter is off us, tossed to the side. I lift my head, looking down at myself and see smeared dirt on my leggings and on the fitted sheet. I'm filthy. What happened?

I can't remember going to bed last night, I don't remember what happened. I slide carefully off Conor, slithering off his body and off the bed. That's when I notice I am not wearing anything but leggings. My shirt and bra are gone.

Walking into the adjoining bathroom, I lean into the shower and turn the water on cold. I slip my leggings and thong off in one go, stepping into the shower. I'm still fuzzy on what happened *yesterday*? I'm not even sure what day it is. How much time has passed.

I raise my face to the flow of water, the snap of the cold water waking me the rest of the way up. I remember the sound of the smashing glass, the man grabbing me, him holding a gun to my head, and that's it.

Pressing my back against the chilled tile, I slide down until my butt is on the floor, sobbing into my hands as the freezing water cascades down, soaking me. I remember being more terrified than I have ever been in my life. I thought I was going to either die or be raped, not sure which would be worse. The play I had with Conor is a totally different feeling than being threatened with the real thing. The attacker made me feel unclean with his comments. I know Dave sent him with his comment of bringing me back. And *him* not wanting me to be touched. This is the second time he tried to take me back, how many more will there be before he finally gets me. I cannot go back, I would rather be dead. Things there will be even worse than they were before.

I draw my legs closer to my body as if I can protect myself. I can't, and it seems no one can. Not even Conor. Dave has too much power and money. I don't care how much money Conor has; he can't compete with Dave.

He doesn't have the influence. He doesn't have the pull Dave has.

Sitting on the floor of the shower, I feel the bite of the hard drops of water on the top of my head and my body. The shower head isn't set on rain shower, it must be set on power. I don't care, I need the hurt to feel. I'm dead inside, so nothing can hurt me after what happened. I should be angry. Ready to do battle with Dave, but instead, I feel nothing. All I need is my body to catch up with my emotions.

I lay my cheek on the top of my knees, crying and sobbing into them, and hear the click as the door opens, and a naked body sits next to me, pulling me into his arms and lap. How can a man like Conor be so vicious and loving? It's as if he's two different men. As if he is who he needs to be at the time.

He has me sideways on his lap, my legs curled around his thighs. "Shit, Savvy. This water is fucking cold. You're a queen if you can stand this. Let me turn it off."

"Nooo. I neeed to feel." My voice shudders with the words, my voice as cold as the water.

"You want to feel? Here." He takes my hand and wraps my fingers around his soft cock. "You feel this. Make me hard enough to fuck you. I'll make you feel like the queen you are." He pulls my head down to his, kissing my lips with everything he has, grinding onto mine, opening mine with his tongue. Conor slightly lifts his head from mine, running his thumb along my bottom lip, his black eyes questioning if it is okay, and I nod. Everything he can do is okay.

The water disappears, and he becomes everything to me. Taking up my sight, my whole vision inside this tiny room is him. He'll be my whole world.

I tug on him as he kisses me with everything he has. As if I'm his whole world. I wish it was true. I wish I could become something to someone. Instead of a thing. A hole to use. A cum toy.

I will use him, too; he will be my security blanket. He's the one always saving me, so he will be my savior, one I will call on when Dave comes again. I know he will. I want someone who will be mine. Eternally mine, and I will use Conor as mine in my mind, even if he eventually finds his own. I am so screwed up in my head, wanting someone who I don't deserve. Who isn't mine and never can be because I am so damaged. But I'll pretend while I can.

Moving my body, I'm now straddling him the best I can, humping my body on his, my pussy along his cock. He groans into my mouth, lifting his lower body up to mine, his pelvis bumps mine.

He slides his hand into my wet hair, tilting my head back with his hand around my throat, thumb against my chin, and devours my lips as if I've become his last meal before his last steps to death. As if I'm his last breath.

He growls into my mouth, and I moan into his. This is what I need to feel, feel as alive as I feel dead right now.

I curl my legs around his back, we are still sitting on the floor of the shower, making out like teenagers. My eyes are heavy with the passion flooding me, he drops his hands to my thighs around him, fingers digging into the skin.

He brings my soul higher than anything, higher than the sun, higher than the stars in the sky. Us together, I feel like I can touch God, I don't need any drug to get high, I only need Conor.

CONOR

Her legs are around my back, and I wrap my hands underneath them. Lifting us off the floor, I carry her into the bedroom, our wet bodies onto the bed. Laying her carefully, I spread her out, legs wide. Her nipples are tight, ready, and waiting for my mouth. I will.

I grip both of her wrists in mine. Leaning down, I suck one nipple into my mouth, suckling her sweet nub, my tongue swirls around, making it as wet as I can. Savvy moans, crying out, her legs trying to rub together, but my body is between them, my knees spreading her legs wider. I want to stretch this out as long as I can, my hard dick will make that more difficult.

I run my knuckles over her bare cunt, leaking with her want. I slap her cunt; her cry is the music I've been waiting to hear. I thrust two fingers deep inside her, and she pushes down, rocking back and forth, trying to fuck herself, but I slap her again in punishment. Not sure about the punishment because my little mouse gets off on the pain. I'm going to try something new when she's about to orgasm, see if that blows it out of this universe.

Running my fingers that had just been in her pussy over her nipples, I spread her juices over them and suck them back into my mouth. Yum. An even better flavor.

I slide my fingers back inside her, adding a third finger, opening her cunt up further for me. Savvy lets out another moan, pushing herself further into my palm. I kiss her on her forehead, her breath catching as I add a fourth finger. I know she can handle it, it's tight, but she needs to be able to handle my dick. It's not small.

"Conor," she breaths my name, raising her hands to her hair and sliding her fingers through it, her head tossing from side to side as I press my thumb against her clit. Removing my fingers, I run them around the hood and into her clit, using my fingernail to flick against the end.

"Plleaaase," she begs.

"Please what?" I ask with an evil chuckle. I love her begging like this. All she wants is her pleasure, and she will get it. After I have mine, then she'll have all the pleasure she wants.

"Please? Come inside me."

I run my nose along the side of her face, whispering into her ear, licking at the shell, "Yes, my little mouse. Don't mind if I do."

Grabbing my dick in my hand, I zero it in on her entrance, shoving it in as hard as I can, my breath catches at how perfect she feels. Like she's my soulmate, she has been meant for me my whole life.

I hammer into her, a jackhammer on overdrive. I don't think I can ever get enough of her. I pull out, rubbing two fingers inside her, getting them good and wet, plunging my dick inside her again. The two fingers I reach to her ass and rub around the rim, but she's so set on how she's feeling right now, she doesn't notice when I slide part of a finger inside her ass.

Our bodies smack together, harder and harder. As we begin building, I can feel my balls get ready to explode. I reach out and grab her throat with a little pressure. She tosses her head back and forth, and I snap our pelvises together again and push her further up onto the bed, pressing harder on her throat, cutting off her air. She grabs my wrist, gasping, arching her neck up more, trying to get better access to breathe, it's not time yet. I press a little harder, and she's clawing again, her beautiful green eyes wide with panic.

They start to close, rolling back into her head, so I let go, and she gasps, coughing. I gather my stamina, pounding into her with all I have, and she cries out. I can feel her fluids gush out of her, and I cum inside her. I hope she gets pregnant; she hasn't asked about birth control, and I haven't seen any pills. She might be getting shots instead. I don't care if she's not. I want her pregnant with my child.

CHAPTER TWENTY-SEVEN

Savannah

I open my heavy eyes, remembering what we did last night. I smile at how I felt cared for, and my heart grows till it feels like it might burst because someone cares for me for the first time in my life. I can't decide which was better, they were so different. The chasing or what we did last night.

Turning my head, expecting to see him still beside me, but instead, he's not there. I slap my hand onto the spot to find it cold, he's been gone for a while, the disappointment overtaking the good feeling I was just wrapped in.

I sit up, sliding out of bed, and use the bathroom, forgoing a shower today. I leave the bedroom and search the house for Conor, but he's nowhere.

There's no one inside. I go to Conor's office where a computer he bought me lies. I open it up to Bay University and go through the online courses I can take for starting in a children's psychology program.

I try to register, but it looks like I have to go there and register. I might even have to go a couple times a week. I don't think Conor will agree to that, he thinks I'm in danger. The front door opens, and I think it's Conor, but Riley appears in the doorway.

"Hey, Riley." The disappointment hits me so hard it's a blow to my chest. I mean, Riley's handsome in a young way, blond hair, blue eyes, boy next door look. I don't think he's over twenty-five, but he's not Conor. Riley doesn't have that confidence Conor has. The life of experience.

"Savannah. What are you doing?" He glances from me to the computer and back again.

I know Conor doesn't want me to leave for my safety, but now, because of his suggestion, I can go to university. I have a fire inside me to start. I hope I'm not late for a new school year. "I need to use a car. Does Conor have an extra one I can use?"

He's shaking his head, and I know I've lost even before I've started. I don't want to wait until he gets home. I want to go now. My brain is buzzing with the excitement of doing something for me. I can now have a life I'm proud of. A life I can finally make something of.

"No, he doesn't want you to leave."

I look hopefully up at him, my face as earnest as I can make it. "He wants me to do something for myself. He told me to take classes. That's what I want to do, sign up for a couple." I hold my hands up together like I'm praying. "Please, Riley. I can't stay locked up with nothing to do. If you go with me?" I mouth *please* again, my eyes wide.

He bites his bottom lip, looking down at his feet and back up at me. He digs into his back pocket, yanking out his phone, and pressing for a contact. He listens as it connects and rings and rings, going to Conor's voicemail. "He told you you could do this?"

I nod as vigorously as I can, my pulse pounds in my ears, hoping he doesn't ask *when* Conor told me this. I'm not going to be stupid and go by myself, although at first, in my excitement, I would have. Now, Riley's stopped me from going off half-cocked. I know someone must go with to protect me.

"Okay, I guess it will be fine if he told you to do it. When do you want to leave?"

I leap off the sofa faster than I have in years, doing an embarrassing bootie dance that has Riley ducking his head and smirking. I'm so happy to be doing something other than cooking, cleaning, and doing Dave's secretarial work. I wouldn't have minded if I hadn't been stuck in the house the rest of the time, he wouldn't let me go anywhere. No friends, nothing.

"Now good for you?" I'm having such a hard time containing myself, it bubbles up as if trying to overflow a bathtub.

"Now's fine. Just remember, don't leave me. Stay by my side." His gaze is so stern it should tone me down, but it doesn't. I want to start the classes now, as soon as I can.

"Okay, let's go."

It doesn't take long to get to Bay University. It's a Monday, so maybe that's why the roads are light or it's an off time. Riley parks the SUV he drove in a visitor spot, watching around us the whole time. He makes me a little nervous the way he's checking any car coming near us. I'm starting to gaze around at anyone, distrustful if they come anywhere near us, thinking they might be suspicious, they might be *the enemy.*

We read the signs and once ask for directions to admissions; it doesn't take long from there. Getting signed up for a few classes takes the longest because I have no records anymore, and I have no clue where my diploma from high school is. They gave me a couple introductory classes and a starter for psychology. They will be both online, and one day a week I have to go to campus for the psychology one. My books are bought, and I'm set to go.

We walk out of admissions, and I'm still bouncing on my sneakers. My first class is online and not till Wednesday, but I'm so excited. I want to shout about it; instead, I hug my books to my chest, making Riley smile at my excitement.

Side-by-side, we walk, silent in our own thoughts. Riley is more relaxed with the laid-back appearance of everyone walking around, doing their own thing. It's quiet and casual here.

We're back in the parking lot and making our way to the SUV, a young man comes up to us. "Hey, can I ask you a question?"

He looks to be about eighteen or even younger, his arms full of books, his face doesn't even look like he's ever had any kind of beard at all. His smile is so hesitant, as if expecting to be kicked like a lost puppy.

"Yes? What do you need?" Riley glares at me, but I'm not going to not help him if I can.

His eyes are wide, his face ingenuous and naïve, I don't see how he could try and hurt us. He doesn't seem capable.

His gaze goes from me to Riley, staying on Riley, chewing on his bottom lip. "I'm really sorry to bother you, but my car broke down." He waves vaguely to his left to a bunch of cars. "I'm broke and need a ride home. I don't have money for a taxi or Uber. My mom had to go to work a half an hour ago, and I'm supposed to be there to babysit my sister." He glances down at his phone, a worried expression on his face.

I glance at Riley, pleading with him as he shakes his head no. I stand staring at him as he continues shaking his head. "No, Savvy. No. Conor will kill me."

"Sure, where do you live?" I answer for Riley as he gapes at me ignoring me. He starts typing furiously on his phone, and I wave at the kid to follow me. He grins at me, frowning worriedly at Riley but follows me to the back seat of the SUV.

"This is such a bad idea," Riley mutters to himself, glancing down at his phone and shaking his head.

153

I mean, he's just a kid, what can go wrong?

CHAPTER TWENTY-EIGHT

Conor

I keep hearing my phone blow up with text messages, but I don't have time to look at them.

I'm busy watching Dave; following him around is my job today. Even with as big as I am, I'm good at staying in the shadows, blending into the people around.

Right now, I'm in the back of a crowd as Dave announces throwing himself into the senate race for California. He actually has a good chance with people only being shown the good guy. The giving guy. The guy who serves at the food bank, helping with the homeless, at the children's hospital, even at the fucking animal shelter.

It's a huge crowd, so it's easy to mingle with the everyday people here. There's at least a hundred people milling about at the West End Park. Mostly blue collar and eating up what he says. The people here wear jeans like me, they are also in t-shirts, tanks or wife beaters, whether dirty from working or clean. Some have logos of the companies they work for as if they were on the way to lunch.

"Everyone, thank you for coming," Dave booms through the crowd on the speakers set up. "I'm sorry my wife isn't here with me to welcome you, but she's feeling under the weather." He winks, his eyes searching the men in the crowd out. "You know what I mean, guys." He chuckles as if it's a joke. There's a half-hearted chuckle from the men, the women only glare at him.

Dave clears his throat, his arrogance falters as his misogynist attitude falls flat. He bolsters himself as only a narcissist can. "I have great ideas for the future of California, and I know you will agree with me, we are the Golden State with our great weather and beaches."

He's losing them again, only he can screw this up with his butchered opinions. His face falls, and he glares at a woman standing behind him and to the side.

She steps forward, "I'm sorry, Mister Collier has to leave. His wife is very ill, and he needs to take care of her."

I burst out a laugh at the idea of Dave taking care of anyone. Looks like this candidate rally has been a bust for him. This is the crown jewel for me.

SAVANNAH

The kid gives us directions to the outskirts of the city where it bumps against the city of Los Angeles itself. The houses are more run down with trash cans littering the streets. I feel bad we're taking him home in this luxurious Caddy. He looks around nervously, and I wonder if he's afraid his neighbors will be jealous.

"Will, your sister is home alone? How old is she?"

"Probably." His head is down, his face distressed at the thought. "She's only five. I've never been late, and Mom will be fired if she is again."

"Riley."

"Yeah, on it," he says, the car shoots forward as Riley follows Will's directions. The house is mowed but the white-painted siding on the house is peeling.

Will throws his door open before the car even stops. "Thanks." He throws over his shoulder as he races up the broken steps leading up to the front door. He doesn't even touch it, and it opens, the house dark and silent. I toss a quick glance at Riley, who he nods, and I hurry after Will, Riley running ahead of me.

I can hear Will's frantic shouts, "Aria. Aria, where are you?" The small house echoes with every word he says as if it's been empty for years.

My pulse races along with my heart as I step into the doorway. There's a torn and battered sofa with dolls strewn throughout the tiny living room. The carpet that might have been white or beige is now brown and bare in spots to the wood floor. On a wobbly, small table, a vase with dying sunflowers have a place of honor in the small front room.

Will is crying now, broken-hearted sobs waft down to us in the front room, the house is a living, breathing ghost of the little girl, and I pray we can find her.

Riley brings Will down the stairs, practically carrying the young man who carries a stuffed dragon in his arms.

His eyes tell me everything. He has given up. "This is her favorite toy. She would have never left it voluntarily," Will says with a broken sob, guilt written all over his face.

"Will," I say his name as gently as I can. "Call your mother. We'll help find her."

CHAPTER TWENTY-NINE

Conor

I'm walking away from the joke of a rally – Dave's going to have to up his game if he wants to win this – and decide to see why my phone was being blown up.

There are five messages and two voicemails from Riley asking what to do about Savannah, that she wants him to take her to Bay University.

My phone buzzes with a call, I pick it up and yell, "What the fuck, Riley?"

"Boss, I called. She said you told her it was okay to register for classes. But there's a problem now."

"Problem?" I start running for my old truck. Didn't want to set myself up in the Rover. "What's wrong? I was looking right at Dave. Did he send someone else? Where are you?" I jam my key in, unlocking the truck, and jump in. "Where are you?"

"Wait. It's not that. There is this kid we met at the college. He said his car wouldn't start, and he needed to get home to his five-year-old sister." He stops. "I know" he says, afraid to tell me more.

"What the fuck, Riley?" I scream, glad I'm inside my truck, but some heads still turn my way to see what the noise was. "Is she okay?"

"Fine. She's fine. It's something else."

His voice cuts out and some words are mumbled, and Savvy cuts in, "It's important, Conor. Come to 1510 Baywood Lane. Please."

I start the truck, my foot pounds on the gas pedal a couple times to get it going. "Riley, you are in big trouble." If he hadn't already known that, I want to be sure he knows he's in deep shit now.

Giving the old truck more gas, I squeal the tires out of the parking lot, people glare at me in response. Like I care.

While I drive, I put the address in the maps app, following the directions as I seethe deep inside, my stomach churning with my frustration. He had one job. One job. To protect Savvy, and what happens? Some kid gets in the way.

I'm considering his punishment as I fly down the freeway, one of those guys weaving in and out, reasonably empty for once. Only late at night and if they're not doing any work on any freeway in Los Angeles for it to be this free of traffic.

The directions take me to the poorer side of town, one I don't come to very often. I make the turns Map says and come to 1510 Baywood Lane. A rundown house trying to make itself look better.

Riley steps out when he sees my truck, a look of fear on his face. Yeah, he better fucking fear what I'm going to do to him. He better hope I don't cut him into tiny pieces for letting her do this.

"Boss, I—"

My fist strikes out before my brain has time to think. I need this right now. Beat the shit out of someone. Riley grunts when my knuckles meet the side of his face, but he stands his ground. I'll give him that, he's not a coward. He will wish he was when I'm done with him. I get ready for a punch with my right hand when a female body thrusts in between us, her arms up wide to protect him.

"It was my idea, Conor."

"What? He doesn't have a mind of his own? He can't follow simple instructions?" I get louder and louder with every word I say until I'm shouting. The pain in my knuckles is nothing compared to the pain in my heart, thinking something bad was happening to Savvy. My right arm is still raised to hit him, I can't with her standing in my way. I have to have some way to hurt someone the way I hurt. I've never felt this way before, and I don't like it.

"Conor. Please. Riley had to do what I told him, otherwise I would have done it on my own." Savvy holds one hand out to me, and I stare down at it. It's delicate like she is. She's not delicate in a physical sense, she can take more than she thinks, but mentally, she is. She doesn't believe in herself enough, should I ruin this for her? She is strong enough to stand up to Riley and now me. I can't crush her newfound strength.

"Okay, what is going on? I will give this the benefit of the doubt. I'll give this a try."

Riley looks relieved, even with blood leaking from the corner of his mouth. Savvy has a thankful expression. I want to do everything I can for her to grow as a woman in her own right. She deserves at least that much.

SAVANNAH

I can't believe Conor agreed to listen to me. I turn my head and look to the house, and Will stands there, scared enough to pee himself, I think.

"Conor, this is Will. Will Perkins. His car broke down, and we gave him a ride here. His five-year-old sister was home alone. We hurried here, but someone took her." I roll my hands together over and over, a nervous habit I know I do. My heart and stomach scrape along the ground, waiting for Conor. He's staring at Will sternly as if he can read his soul from his face.

"So, where is she?"

"No one knows, that's why she's missing." Why doesn't he get it? He still stares at Will, who is starting to become unglued at his seams. His body shakes, and his lips are making a weird motion.

"Show me." Conor glares at Riley, expecting him to tell him everything. I will, this is me standing up for myself.

"Follow me." I swivel and stride back inside the little house and up the small flight of stairs to the little girl's bedroom. There's not much here. A tiny mattress on the floor, a lot of dust I hadn't noticed before. A couple discarded toys, and that's it. Where are her clothes? I don't see a closet or even a dresser or anything.

Conor growls behind me, I tip my head to glance at him. He's even angrier than before. I have a strange feeling. "Where's the kid? Riley." He booms through the small house, I'm afraid he is going to blow it down with how loud he is shouting.

He bounds down the stairs, taking all five at once. There is something weird going on here, I just can't see what it is, it is just out of reach for me to grasp.

"Where's the kid!" Conor's hands open and close at his sides, and he's breathing heavily through his flared nostrils like a bull.

"He-he was just here a second ago." Riley backs up, realizing he's screwed up again. Real terror appears on his face. A terror that runs throughout your body, freezing your organs and movements.

"Riley." Conor's teeth are clenched, and the word is strained as if he is having a hard time restraining himself.

"He was just here. I swear." He races to the street, looking up and down each way, frantic and panicking in every turn of his hopeful head to see the kid. "There he is."

Riley runs down the street to the right, jumping over a fence and flying over another. "Fuck. Come back, you little shithead."

Conor is right behind; the neighborhood is now standing in the street and on their front stoops, their phones out, recording everything. I don't know what to do or say, I've never handled anything like this before. I have a feeling this is going to be bad. Very bad for all of us.

CHAPTER THIRTY

Conor

Riley has the kid Will; if that's his real name, I'm going to find out what is going on. What is truth and what is lies, and I think it is all lies. Heads will roll, maybe literally, in the end.

I grab this kid, who I think is older than he says, by the back of his shirt, hauling him over to me. His face is level with mine, his feet hanging a few inches off the ground.

"What did you do?" I shake his hanging body, my lips pulling back in a snarl. I want him to see and feel my fury. In fact, I'm beyond furious. I'm *way beyond* furious. I'm a heat-seeking missile about to explode.

"I-I-do-n't know what you mean. My sister."

"You don't have a sister," I snarl. I want to tear him to pieces with my teeth and bare hands.

"Riley, I want you to search the Caddy from top to bottom. There was some reason he wanted to be with you." I jerk my head to look behind me, sighing in relief to find a panting Savvy, bent over, hands on knees, fine ass staring at me. Seeing her in this position makes my unruly dick jump to attention. I don't need this now. I don't want the image of her bent over, her hands spreading her ass cheeks wide apart for me. The image almost brings me to my knees, it's so graphic. The pain is unimaginable. I squeeze my eyes shut for a second to steel my mind from her un-angelic temptation.

The residents of the area have their phones recording, so I drag Will along with me, he's stuttering, trying to convince me he didn't do anything wrong. He's the victim. Yeah, right. Being a cop, I've learned to read liars easily.

One hand on the back of his shirt, the other around his arm, yanking him along as he tries to slow his forward motion, I march him ahead of me, stumbling, stiff, arms and legs ungainly.

I give the people with their cameras a smile to show I have no fear of their social media posting. I'm not hurting him, no one knows who he is. I'm positive he doesn't live here.

The three of us make it back to where his house was supposed to be, Riley brings his upper body out of the SUV, turning his head to look at us. He nods at me, holding up a cell phone.

"Savvy, you ride with Riley. You. You ride with me." I have handcuffs in the glove box of my truck and lead him over, forcing the cuffs on tight, with hands behind his back, making sure they click on tight enough to pinch his skin. I shove him into the passenger seat, snapping the shoulder harness on as tight as the hand cuffs. He's not going anywhere.

I get in the truck, start the engine, and looking over my shoulder, back out onto the street, Riley right behind.

We cruise back to my house, the guy, who I'm not sure is even named Will, I will take down to the basement and interrogate him until he gives me the answers I want. If he doesn't have the answers, then, well.

He sobs, "why, why," over and over so much I'd like to kill him right now. I must have those answers. I don't talk to him, I don't communicate in any way. I drive. I keep glancing in the rear-view mirror, making sure the Caddy behind me is safe.

I bite the inside of my bottom lip and tsk to myself. There's a plain black car behind them. Like a cop car, but it doesn't have any sirens on it or the spotlights. That doesn't mean it's not.

I hit the contacts in the Rover and ask, "Reel, are you there?" I wait for him to answer.

"Yeah, I'm here. What do you need?"

"Two things. There's a car following me. Not sure if it's the police. Need you to check on it. Also, I need you to check up on someone. Will? Is that your first name? And your last and middle?"

"No, I'm William Charles Prescott." He seems more together.

"So, you gave a fake last name before, huh?" My tone is as disgusted as it can get.

"Reel, I need everything you got ASAP. I want to know if those are cops or pretending," I say, my eyes shift from Will to the Caddy, to the car behind them, back to the road, and start again, all within seconds.

"Will do, boss man." I frown at the way he says that. It's the mocking tone, I don't know what that is for.

I hit the end call, more than a little irritated with everything. I have no idea what Dave's end game is beyond getting Savvy back. I do know he needs his wife for his election. I can't figure out what else he wants.

Leading my small, two-car caravan on a roundabout way with the third car following us, I now know it is us they are after. Since they continue to follow me down roads no one would have a real reason to be on, I decide to go back home. They must know who I am and where I live, so there is no reason to hide it. I know Riley must be confused as to why the circuitous way I'm driving. Maybe not because I'm sure he saw the car behind him.

All of this shit is pissing me the fuck off. I hate not being able to see ahead of what might happen next. I lead us back to my estate, wanting to find out what the black car will do when we get there.

I pull up to the gate, it immediately opening at the first sight of my truck. I lead the cars through, the black sedan close behind Riley. I slam the brakes, more pissed off than before, and throw open my door. "Stay." I point at his face and tell Will with the tone of correcting a bad dog.

"I'm not going anywhere," he mutters under his breath to me, throwing a glare as if proving some kind of point.

Slamming the door harder than need, I strut over to the black car, Riley right behind me. A few seconds later, a few more of my men appear, surrounding me. I recognize the two men. One is Erik, a detective I've worked with once or twice, the other is Axel. I've only seen him around the station.

"Why are you guys following us, Erik?" No need to beat around the so-called bush.

He saunters up to me, his hands in the front pockets of his slacks, he rocks back onto his heels. Erik is trying to work his way to the fast track to the chief's job when he eventually retires. Erik is mid-thirties, I think. Still young. Brash. Hard-headed, thinks he knows everything. "Look, Conor."

He rolls back onto the balls of his feet and takes a couple steps closer, his hand plops onto my shoulder. "I don't know what's going on with the three of you." He jerks his chin to Savvy. "I don't want to get involved, but Dave called the chief, and we were assigned this."

I nod, pretending I understand. Inside, I'm seething, my insides a conflagration of intense fire. "So, this is official, even if you're not using an official vehicle."

"Well, not officially official," Erik says, and I shrug his hand off.

The other cop, Axel, barges toward us, his jowly, bulldog face squinting a glare at me. "Look, asshole. Give the girl up. What is she to you but a convenient fuck?"

I meet him head on. My chest pressing hard against his, each of us not wanting to give an inch or even a quarter of an inch.

"Guys." Savvy's voice next to me makes me draw back. "You can tell my ex I'm never going back. There is nothing he can do to make me go back to his abusive ass."

"That is an erroneous theory," Axel spouts with all the pompous attitude he can muster, the loose fat in his neck jiggles as he shakes his head.

"Uh. No, it's not." Savvy glares at him, not backing down or acting submissive like she would have days ago. I am proud of her.

"What's your proof? X rays? Doctor's reports?" Axel counters. "You have no proof for your accusations."

Something hits me over the head hard enough to sink through my anger. "The chief doesn't know about this. That's why you're in this car instead of official business. Dave paid you off. Right? How much to lose your dignity and libel slander. You do know I can meet him dollar for dollar and win. I'll find out everything and bring myself to the chief. You have no idea who you're dealing with. I will ruin you." They think they know me; they haven't met the real me. They've only met the Conor I want everyone to see.

A car door slams, and a female voice joins in, "Savannah. What is going on here?"

Savvy turns her head to look at the woman, her jaw drops, and her eyes widen. "Mom?"

CHAPTER THIRTY-ONE

Savannah

"Mom?" I'm in total shock at her being here. I've haven't seen her since I got married. They never visited me once. My father was still alive then, it's as if once I was gone, I was forgotten. I called, but the calls were never returned.

"Why are you here?" The shock still floods my body and mind, I can't think of any questions. It's frozen in a block of blank ice.

She walks toward me, looking down her straight nose at me. We look nothing alike. She's blond where I have dark hair. She has blue eyes where mine are green. She's tall where I'm average. Avery Holland is everything I'm not. Confident. Elegant. Polished.

"Why are you here with this. This. Person?" She sneers up her nose at Conor. Until I left home at eighteen, she always made me feel small and insignificant, I know the look well. She doesn't bother him; he ignores her like she's irrelevant. He does look rough, dressed in jeans and a hoodie with all his tattoos on display.

My heart pounds in my chest, a wild bird beating its body and wings against the bars of my ribcage. Not in fear or nervousness. No, it is anger. For the first time, I feel defensive fury, which I unleash against her.

"I'm certainly not going to be with that abusive asshole Dave. I'm done with him. I'll never go back out of my free will. Never," I yell at her like I never have before.

"You ungrateful bitch," she sneers back, her eyes looking me up and down as if I disgust her, dismissing me. "After the way I *took care of you*. And you were not my child. You were out of an affair your father had with a whore."

I gasp and draw back, my head feeling like it might explode at this. I don't know how to feel about this news and can't believe she's not my mother, but I understand now why she has never cared for me. I mean I would never do that to any child. Even if the child wasn't my own.

She grabs me by my arm, pulling me closer, her red talons digging into my skin, leaving bruises, I'm sure. "You should have died along with your slut of a mother." Avery, I can't call her Mom now, raises her other arm, reaching out to slap me, but a male hand grabs hers into his. Squeezing it in a tight grasp. Avery cries out, and he lets go.

"Did you see what he did? He hurt me." Fake tears pour from her eyes, a sob as fake as the tears wrenched from her throat.

Erik storms over to Conor, hauling him close so he can spit, "This is it, fucker. I'm taking you to see the chief."

Conor chuckles as if he heard a good joke. "Yeah, we'll see what he says about this if I even get there."

"What does that mean? What are you fucking thinking of accusing us of?" Erik's hands are on his hips, he thrusts his chest out, showing how important he thinks he is. Conor continues laughing at him, pissing him off even more. "Turn around, Conor. You're under arrest."

"You really want to ruin your career this way, Erik?" He shakes his head as if truly disappointed in him. "I'll go with to get this over with. But you're not putting handcuffs on me."

"Conor." I don't know what to say to him. I don't want him to leave me alone with the woman who I thought was my mother, now I know my mother died giving birth to me. I don't believe my father had an affair. There must have been something more going on. I don't believe it. There is nothing about it anyway.

He walks over, taking me into his arms, pulling me close, and kissing me as if it will be our last. That I don't believe. He grinds his teeth against mine, his tongue thrusts against mine as if he's fucking me.

Conor finally pulls away, me gasping for the breath I lost in our graphic kiss. Our lips barely touch as he whispers, "I'll have Riley watch over you and make sure no one," he turns his head to glare a narrow gaze at m-Avery, "I mean, no one will harm you."

"I know. Come back soon."

"I won't be gone long. Unless he has the chief in his pocket as well." A shadow of doubt crosses his face like a dark cloud before he brightens and says, "I'll call Riley right away and have him send a car for me."

Conor steps away and says to Avery, "You better not hurt her in any way."

She gasps with a thin, skeletal hand to her flat chest. "He threatened me. You heard him."

"He didn't threaten you, Avery." I sigh, so tired of her nonsense. She has always wanted all the attention for herself.

"I'm your mother, Savannah," she hisses at me, sounding exactly like the snake in the grass she is. "Call me Mother."

"You've treated me like an unwanted puppy my whole life, just told me you're not my mother, and now you want me to call you Mother?" I screech at her, my whole body vibrating with the pain and fury I have no other way to let out.

Everyone here is watching the sordid drama of my life unfold like a reality TV drama. The guards with their mouths open looking at Conor for instructions, the detectives not knowing how to proceed, Conor and Riley wanting to protect me from this but not being able to.

"This is you all the time, Savannah. Drama, drama, drama. You didn't come to my school play," she mocks in a high-pitched voice. "I don't have a birthday party for my friends." She pushes her face closer to me. So close I can see the red streaks in her blood shot eyes up and personal, and the tiny hairs on her chin she tries to pluck out. "Let me tell you, you little, fat cow. You didn't have any friends," she shrieks, showing her true personality. "You need to go back to your husband."

"Why do you keep shoving getting back with Dave in my face?" I run my hand through my hair over the top of my head, yanking on the strands at the ends. I'm so frustrated. I wish throwing a tantrum would solve everything, I would do it for a little calm. I have a new life I want to lead. My life. However that life looks.

But why does she want me back with him so bad? What do they have to do with each other? And why is this happening to Conor? Are bad things going to continually happen to him because he's helping me? Is this all because of me, somehow?

Maybe I should leave, all I'm doing is causing him problems.

CHAPTER THIRTY-TWO

Conor

I know Riley's with her, protecting her, but I feel it is my job I'm failing on. Sitting in the back of the car while Erik and Axel sit in front, I drum my fingers against my thigh as I wait to find out what's going on and whether it's Dave shitting on me. My anger issues are at an all time high, flowing hot through me like magma straight to the top of my head, blowing the top off like a volcano.

It doesn't take long to reach the station, and as the men escort me inside, I get yelled greetings, clapping of hands on my shoulders that I'm back since I've been off work when Savvy came to live with me, which pisses the two men off. I guess they are not so happy I'm well liked.

The long walk through the bullpen, past the desks, to the end of a long hallway to the chief's office. Erik knocks on the door and waits, then the command to enter.

Erik's hand on my back shoves me into the room, making me stumble. I turn my head to glare at him, it should have made him burn to a crisp on the spot with the anger rushing through my veins.

Chief Edward Collins looks at us from behind his desk. Axel reaches out, closing the blinds on the window. For some reason, he doesn't want anyone to see. They want this, whatever this is, to be a secret.

"Men, what's going on?" He gazes questioningly from one to the other.

Before the other two can say anything, I do, "No idea, Chief. They act like I'm some kind of criminal." I give the chief my most engaging smile. "I was just getting home when they accosted me. Threatened me."

Chief Ed and I are almost friends, he's about my age, and we've known each other since we were beat cops, we try to keep the friendship more workplace so there's no reason to say preferential treatment for me. Ed is a stern but fair chief. I think this nonsense will be over soon, so I can get back to Savvy and get the business with Will taken care of. I hope Riley put him in the basement under lock and key.

The room is silent except for our heavy breaths.

"Chief," Erik starts. "Conor is doing some underhanded dealings. He has kidnapped Dave Collier's wife and is keeping her at his house."

I raise my eyebrows, flying them to the top of my head. I can't believe they are trying that. I knew Dave was involved. "Go on. Let us hear your fable."

"It is no lie. Dave called me, worried about his wife." Erik glowers with a death stare at me. He's going all the way with this story, it seems.

Ed sets his elbows on his desk, weaving his fingers together, his two pointer fingers touching, tapping together as he frowns. "Conor, what's going on? Is this true?"

"No, Chief. I went to Dave's office a week ago or so and found bruises on Savvy-um-Savannah's face. I wanted to take them out to lunch, but Dave said he was too busy and to take her. So, I did." I walk around and sit in one of the chairs since this might be a long conversation.

"Go ahead. Have a seat." Ed waves a hand at me in mockery, and the other two sit in the other chairs.

"She said she forgot something at the office and wanted me to stop by there. Dave had told her to take the rest of the day off. Anyway, she was gone for a while, and I decided to see what was taking so long. Dave was going to slap her. He had his pants around his ankles with his dick in a young woman who was crying. She eventually said she hadn't wanted to have sex with him, but his money talked, and she went to his office. I think she was underage, but she left, and it can't be proved." I lean on the arm of the chair, my body forward.

Ed leans back in his chair, contemplating my story.

"He just said he can't prove it. I don't know what this has to do with anything," Axel protests, indignation and distrust in every line on his plump face.

"Anything else, Conor?" Ed asks, wanting me to give him more proof. I don't think he's in on it, I can't trust anyone here right now.

"Yeah, I went to Dave's house later. I had a bad feeling. He had left the front door slightly open and was hitting Savannah. I took her away, and he's been fighting to get her back. She doesn't want to go. She wants a divorce." I sit back and wait for the decision on my story. If I have to quit, that's what I'll do.

Ed studies my face. He has an uncanny way of telling whether someone is telling the truth or not. That's what makes him such a good chief of police, that and the fact he's fair.

I study Erik and Axel, and they look nervous, fidgeting in their chairs. Like they're not sure they will be believed or not. I don't think Ed will fall for their story, but you never know.

Ed stands, walking around the desk until he's in front of it. He sits on the edge, the palms of his hands flat on the top of the desk, crossing his legs at the ankles, staring at each one of us for a long time.

When he gets to Axel, he caves. "Chief, you can't believe him. She's Dave's wife. She was kidnapped. He talked her into it."

Axel rubs his hands up and down his pants, his breaths quicken, and he won't look Ed in the eyes, all signs he's lying. He's so nervous sweat beads on his face, pouring from his forehead into his eyes and into the deep wrinkles of his face. Ed doesn't say anything, only stares at him. Waiting. For him to break. It doesn't take long.

"I'm sorry. I'm sorry. Erik talked me into it," Axel whines, his eyes shooting from Ed to Erik, and he jumps to his feet. Shaking his fist at Axel, Erik growls, "You lying sack of shit. You were into this as much as me." He turns his head to Ed, tic jumping in his tight jaw. "She's still Dave's wife."

Ed looks from Erik to me. "She doesn't want Dave. She doesn't have to stay with him." Ed turns his attention back to both of the other men. "You are both fired."

CHAPTER THIRTY-THREE

Savannah

I bite the nail on my pointer finger of my left hand, a spark of pain as my front teeth bite into the skin of the nail bed and a sliver of blood leaks. My gaze flashes to the door I can't see through. We left him alone with the two detectives. Riley rushed Will and me inside, going back out to stand with the other guards protecting the house.

It's been an hour, and they're still out there. I should be thankful they are protecting me, but I'm so worried about Conor. Worried he will go to jail or be fired. Jail I guess would be worse for him with all the men he has put in there.

I feel like I'm a refugee in a war with no home, nowhere to go, cast out, other than staying with others. Instead of weapons and blood, I'm left with vicious words, bruises, and broken bones.

Will went upstairs looking for a room, I still don't know if him having a younger sister is the truth or not. I'm thinking not because I now know what Conor saw. Now as I think back, I see what we missed. That house has not been lived in for a while. I can't believe we hadn't seen it at the time, but it had been a frantic, screaming mess at the time, and the lawn had been mowed recently. Those toys must have been props Will or someone else left. We still need to get more information out of him. It might have to wait till Conor gets back.

I'm in the middle of the foyer, not knowing what to do, and the door opens. Riley and another guard I recognize walk in, talking and gesturing wildly. They walk right by me as if I'm a ghost. They walk down the hall to a room Riley has a key to and go inside.

What is in there? Do I even want to know? I creep forward as quietly as I can, trying to be the ghost they ignored me as. I hear some banging, and Riley comes out first, the other guard seconds later.

Riley jumps when he sees me, shoving the door closed after they both exit with a loud slam. "Why are you here, Savannah?"

"What's in there?" I stare at the door as if it will show me what's inside. I'm becoming more curious the longer I'm here. Before, I never wanted to know what Dave was up to, it only caused beatings. Now, my life is becoming easier, and the new freedoms is something I'm still getting used to.

"Nothing." He turns back to the door, his key locking it again. I watch as the keychain disappears back into his pocket.

"So, why are you keeping *nothing* locked up?" I'm persistent, if nothing else, my eyes jumping from the door to his face and back again. I'm so curious. It must be important.

"It's Conor's stuff. If he wants it locked up, it is." His tone is final, and he holds his hand out to go before him. He wants to be sure I don't pick the lock or something. The thought makes me giggle to myself. As if I knew how. Savannah Collier, master thief. That thought makes me giggle even harder, and both Riley and the other guard look at me as if I'm a nutcase. I might be with everything that has happened to me so far the past eighteen years.

I walk ahead of them, standing at the bottom of the staircase staring up. What about Will? I don't want them to remember him if they forgot, but I want to know what he knows.

"I'm going upstairs. Let me know when Conor calls. I want to go with when you pick him up." I don't look at him, I don't want him to think I'm planning something. Well, I am, but nothing bad, I just want to pick Will's brain. I walk up the stairs, not looking back, knowing both men are watching me. The hairs on the back of my neck and skin tingle in the way it does when you know you're being watched behind your back.

I'm at the top of the curving staircase and turn the corner to the right instead of the left, not sure which room he decided to pick. I stop at each door, knock lightly twice, and when no one answers, go to the next. I lift my hand to knock and see the door is slightly open an inch. I push, it opens further, and I hear music and singing. A beautiful tenor voice sings a ballad that's both touching and hard to hear. It's so tender.

"Will." I hate to interrupt whatever recording he's listening to on his phone, but we must have this conversation.

He hurries out of the bathroom, his hair mussed and dry. He hasn't taken a shower yet. He stops dead when he sees me, his face is the dark red of a beet as he rubs his hand against the back of his neck. "Um, wha...what are you doing here?"

"We have to talk. Was that the radio you were listening to?" His beet face is running to his ears and down his neck. Why is he so embarrassed?

"Uh, yeah, it was."

"What station? Who is the artist? It was so beautiful and moving." I'd like to know who sang it, I want the song or album if there is one.

"Oh, ah, I don't know. I didn't pay attention." He's being so sketchy about this. I don't understand why, that's not what's important right now.

"Okay, anyway, why did you say your sister was kidnapped? Why did you lie like that?"

He turns away from me, his body stiff and jerky as he runs his hand over his hair. "I'm sorry. I-I didn't feel I had a choice. I don't have a sister." Will swivels back to me so fast, grabbing my arms in his hands, bumping me against the wall, his face twisting with his anguish. For a minute, I get scared and my stomach drops, but I see he doesn't want to hurt me, he wants me to understand. "It's just my mother and me. I'm telling the truth, this time. She works two jobs so I can go to the university. I work as much as I can, but I have a full load of classes to do to graduate. She feels if I finish early like I did in high school, it will benefit us better."

"Will, it's okay. Really. Just tell me the truth."

"I don't know how he found me or how he knew we were so desperate for money." His face is tight and worried. I'm sure about what's going to happen to him later.

"Who was it?" I twist my arms out of his hands and slip underneath his arm to stand beside him. I don't like being restrained like that unless Conor does it, for some reason. If only I understood my relationship with Conor. If we have a relationship at all. It's just so confusing.

"I-I don't know." His face is scrunching in confusion.

"He never said his name. Only gave me addresses and names." He rams his back against the wall, his head in his hands, shaking it back and forth. "He would meet me in a Benz and hand me an envelope with the promised money. That's it. My mother will be so ashamed of me when I tell her."

I rub my hand over his drooping back, I don't know why I'm the one comforting him. He's just a kid. "Do you remember anything about the license plate?"

He scrunches his eyes as he tries to remember. "I think it started with a C. A personal plate."

My heart stops beating for a millisecond as I freeze. Really? It's that easy? "Could it have been Collier?"

"Maybe. I only saw the first letter by the way he parked. I wish I could help more, Savannah." He is bent forward, almost bowing to me, his hands pressing together like he is praying.

"What's going on here?" Conor growls, as pissed as a man can be.

CHAPTER THIRTY-FOUR

Conor

Chief let me leave, he held on to Erik and Axel, interviewing them to see if they are going to prison for taking bribes. I don't care about them anymore; they are in a hell of their own making. All I care about is getting to Savvy. No one is picking up their phones. Luckily, I had my credit card in my wallet and phone so can Uber home. No thanks to anyone there. Heads might roll. Literally.

I hop into the ride and sit forward, not being able to wait until the car stops. He's starting to turn into the drive before the gate, and I jump out while the car is still rolling forward. I had added a big tip to the order, so no worries about that. The guard hits the button for the gate the second he recognizes me, I don't even care who he is. I only want to see Savvy, my new obsession. My dick is so hard thinking about seeing her. I know it has only been a couple hours. I can't help it, I'm obsessed.

As I run onto my property, the men run after me, yelling God knows what, not that I care, all I want or need is to see Savvy.

Touch her.

Fuck her.

Make sure she's safe.

To me, it has been forever since I've seen her, I know it has only been, at the most, a couple hours. That's the way obsession is, I guess.

I need her in my arms. I need to hold her, keep her safe. Make sure she stays safe. Is that love? I don't think love is the all-consuming lust and desire to shelter her from harm I feel.

"Boss. Boss," Riley calls as I run past him as if demons are after me. I might be one of them.

"Where is she?" I whirl around and grab him by one shoulder, holding tight enough he should be wincing in pain; instead, his face is stoic and straight.

"Upstairs. Boss, she's getting curious. Asking questions. I'm not sure how long I can hold her off for. You need to tell her."

"Tell her what? There is nothing to tell her. The only reason you know is there has to be someone here with all these extra men I can trust." I lean closer, my face right up against his. "I can trust you, Riley. Right?" My left hand goes to my gun, but I had given it to him before Erik or Axel could take it from me. He reaches behind his own back and pulls out my gun, handing it to me. He reaches back again, pulling out his own gun and handing that to me as well.

"This is how much you can trust me, Conor."

I eye him, waiting a few minutes, and my phone rings. I pick it up, seeing it's Reel. Haven't talked with him in a while. "Reel."

"You can trust him, Conor. I picked him just for you." His voice comes from one of the cameras in the room. I don't know how he gets into the electronics. It's almost supernatural.

"There's so much going on right now, Reel. How do I know I can trust you?" I'm so fucking in my own head; I don't know who is whom. Or who I can trust.

I'm going to have to give him the benefit of the doubt, I have no choice, I can't do it all myself. White noise rushes through my head as my mind races around one scenario after another. I come up blank with each one. There are so many variables to each one, and I can't pick one that will work. Life is unstable and fickle, someone or something can come and fuck the whole plan up.

I go to my office, over to my desk, and sit, waking my computer up. I wait the few minutes needed and click on cameras in the hallways. I watch Savvy climb the stairs to the second floor, turning right to an unused section. She knocks on each door, waits a few seconds, and walks to the next door. When she gets to the fifth, she stares at it and pushes it open, walking inside. I switch through the cameras until I find the room, and Will walks out of the bathroom.

He has no shirt on, my blood bubbles and boils in my veins that he's standing in front of her half-naked. I jerk to a stand like a marionette, they start talking, and I turn the speaker on.

"What station? Who is the artist? It was so beautiful and moving."

"Oh, ah, I don't know. I didn't pay attention."

I must have come in the middle of their conversations; I continue to listen to find out what Will's story is and how I can use him to get to Dave because *I know he is involved.*

"Okay, anyway, why did you say your sister was kidnapped? Why did you lie like that?"

"I'm sorry. I-I didn't feel I had a choice. I don't have a sister." I already knew that. He turns, grabbing Savvy's arms in his hands, pushing her against the wall. I howl in outrage at the sight, my hands wide, ready to tear him to pieces. He starts talking again when I reach the door. "It's just my mother and me. I'm telling the truth this time. She works two jobs so I can go to the university. I work as much as I can, but I have a full load of classes to graduate early. She feels if I finish early like I did in high school, it will benefit us better."

"Will, it's okay. Really. Just tell me the truth."

"I don't know how he found me or how he knew we were so desperate for money."

She twists herself away from him, standing beside him instead.

"I-I don't know." He pauses for a minute as if collecting his thoughts. "He never said his name. Only gave me addresses and names." I'm watching this like a disaster movie, my fists on the desk, I'm bent down, frothing at my mouth, my heart in my throat. Will leans his back against the wall, his head in his hands, shaking it back and forth. "He would meet me in a Benz and hand me an envelope with the promised money. That's it. My mother will be so ashamed of me when I tell her."

She rubs her hand against his naked skin, and my blood starts to boil again. What the fuck is she thinking? "Do you remember anything about the license plate?"

"I think it started with a C. A personal plate."

"Could it have been Collier?"

"Maybe. I only saw the first letter by the way he parked. I wish I could help more, Savannah."

At his saying her name, I'm already out the door, jumping up the steps three at a time, reaching the door to the room before he can draw another breath. I've never run so fast or so hard to get to her. I've never had this kind of reason before.

"What's going on here?" I ask, my lips lift in a snarl, the feral animal alive in me.

I grab her into my arms, one around her back, the other under her knees. I carry her down the hall, stomping my boots, making sure everyone knows where I'm taking her. "Riley," I yell with a roar. I hear pounding footsteps, and he appears beside me, panting.

"Make sure he doesn't leave his room until I say so."

"Got it, boss." I can feel his gaze on us as I kick the master bedroom door open and kick it closed. It bounces back open, the latch broken. I toss her into the middle of the bed. Turning, I close the door with a fragile calm I don't feel. I don't hear the click of the latch, but I know no one will dare bother me. They know it will cost them their life.

CHAPTER THIRTY-FIVE

Savannah

I'm tossed on the bed and stunned for a moment. Conor's face is tight and wild-looking. A beast on the lookout for its mate. And he's found it.

He turns away from the door, growling under his breath, "Don't touch another man like that. He wasn't wearing a shirt." He stalks toward me, placing one foot carefully and silently at a time. He's terrifying and panty-melting, the way he's watching me. It shouldn't turn me on the way he does. Dominant. Protective. Practically marking his territory. He should lift his leg and pee on me when another man is around. The thought of him doing just that makes a giggle burst out with a snort. "Take your clothes off."

A smirk lifts one tip of his mouth, an evil spark glittering in his eyes. I don't know what he's thought of, I'm sure it's good. I'm not afraid with him. I never will be now. Dave always, but Conor is slowly teaching me to stand up for myself. I'm important. I shouldn't let myself be downgraded just to make someone else feel bigger about themselves.

I watch in fascination as his strong, thick, workman fingers unbutton his shirt. One at a time. If I didn't know any better, I'd think he was doing a strip tease. I start shimmying my leggings off and lift my shirt over my head, watching as he finishes undressing, too.

"So, what do you want me to do to you today, little mouse?" He takes a step closer to the bed, and I notice that my jaw hangs open. I swipe at my lips to make sure there is no drool at the corners.

I clear my throat, not sure I'm able to speak with all the lust clogging my esophagus, my panting breaths gasping, "Whatever you want."

He throws his head back and laughs. "Oh, you don't want to say that. I have so many ideas. How do you feel about...." He walks closer to the side where I'm lying. Leaning down until his mouth is closer to my ear. "Being tied up, mouth duct taped and choked."

Why do his words make my pussy pulse and flood?

"Do you want me to use rope or handcuffs? Hmm? Duct tape or ball gag?" His breath swirls against my cheek, warming the inside of my ear, making me shiver.

He bites the lobe of my ear, chuckling darkly. "No answer? I'll do it all. Hmmm. Ball gag or duct tape. I have a lot of that, the gag is new and still in its packaging. I'll do that next time. Turn over." A sharp pain makes me squeal, and I realize he slapped my butt.

I lift my head to tell him my opinion of him spanking my rear, but words fail me. I've seen him naked a few times now, and every time I'm stunned by how masculine he is. He should be a model with how sexy he is.

My jaw drops and moves, but no words come out. I have none, all I want to do is jump on the boner he's sporting in his tight jeans.

He lowers his body until he's planking over mine, hands fisted on either side of my head, and I stop breathing at how sexy this is.

His lips are barely a breath away from mine when someone knocks on the door. "What the fuck," he shouts so loud the chandelier on the ceiling shudders.

"Boss. I hate to disturb you, but the kitten needs to be fed." Riley sounds like it's something he really hates doing. I want to laugh, but it's not funny. Well, maybe a little.

I move my hand to nudge at Conor's shoulder. "It's okay, Riley," I say.

"I can feed him again. I fed him a little while ago," Riley offers. I guess he probably has an idea about what we're doing.

"Thank you." Conor is so grudging in his thanks, it's like watching a dark comedy. He glares at me. "Not funny."

"It is a little." I try to keep the smile off my lips, but it's difficult, and I can feel the ends of my mouth twitch at a smile.

"I see that. I think you deserve a spanking for disobeying me." It's his turn to smile, his is darker, deeper, more devastating in its promise of dark desires of punishment to become fulfilled.

I nod furiously, not sure what the punishment will be. My mind says no, but my body is saying hell yes. I watch his face; his eyes darken to the color of burning coals as his pupils expand in his desire for me. I feel a sharp pain and gasp, looking down as he spanks my pussy again. But. I like it. The temporary pain leaves a rapturous tingling, leaving my body stiff and unable to move as a surge takes over, and my heart takes a giant leap up.

"You seem to like that punishment. They're not supposed to be enjoyed. I'll have to do something about that. Now turn over," he growls, his voice as thick as my brain feels. Conor helps me move since I don't have the brainpower to move my own body.

I'm on my front now, he grabs my arms, yanking them behind my back, cold metal being attached to my wrists. They are loose enough to not hurt, tight enough to give a slight bite. I definitely know they are there.

"Good?" he asks, his hands lightly running up and down my arms, the callouses on his fingers scraping against my skin, leaving prickles and goosebumps behind. My breaths come faster as I'm growing more breathless with every pass of his touch. I close my eyes, not being able to keep them open, they are so heavy it feels like weights are attached to them.

He gives my rear a sharp, hard smack. "Open your eyes. I know you've closed them."

I lift my cheek off the pillow, blinking my heavy eyes, too overcome from the most intense orgasm I've ever had.

I try to look over my shoulder at him to show him I've done what he's wanted.

"Good girl," he praises. I should be offended, I'm not a dog, but something about him doing it makes it okay. I've always been submissive and want to be strong now, but the way he praises me like he truly means it makes flutters flurry through my stomach. I don't mind being submissive to Conor, it gives me pleasure to give him pleasure.

He spreads my legs even wider than they were when I changed positions. Lying between them, he spreads my folds, starting on my clit. I can't see what he's doing from my position, and I feel two fingers being forced inside. I know I'm still tight from the years of not having sex, he's getting me ready as carefully as he can.

I cry out as he pumps his fingers in and out, and he teases, "Quiet. You don't want Riley to hear, do you?"

Shaking my head no, I cry out again in disappointment when he removes his fingers from me. "Here, let's make sure you keep quiet. I have some tape in the bedside table. Duct tape is good for anything."

CONOR

I slip my fingers out of her, moving away to the nightstand closest to me and the bed, opening the drawer I want. In it, I have odds and ends, duct tape, screwdrivers, and other stuff. I pick up the roll and scoot back over to her, running my hand over her plump ass. I love her ass. I want in that hole so badly, but that will have to wait for another time. I'll have to train that hole. It'll take time to open her up.

She has a freckle on each ass cheek, right on the curve, and I want to bite each one. I think I will. First, keep her from screaming, I think she would be embarrassed if Riley could hear her. I won't mind, make sure he knows who she belongs to. I measure out a length, cut it with my teeth, and measure out another portion.

Leaning back over her, I pull her limp head back up by her hair and place one of the tape lengths over her mouth and the other right above. I press down on them making sure she can't open her mouth.

She tries to moan but nothing comes out. Perfection. I lay her cheek back on the pillow and go back to playing with her body like the toy she wants to be for me. She's the perfect submissive. Yielding and ready to learn to give herself over to me.

I thrust three fingers in hard and fast, getting her to push back when I pull out. I take two of the fingers that were in her cunt and slowly put them in her ass. Her head shakes back and forth, her body trying to worm away. I won't let her and rest my other hand on the middle of her back, holding her in place. I ease my way in until they are all the way. I moan at the sight as her body sucks my fingers in. And pull out and back in. Out. In. I watch as her ass opens, sucking my fingers in, wishing it was my dick, and I add the third finger when she moans again. I can come right now, like this, all over her ass. I release her and finger her clit, getting her ramping back up again. I'm going to make sure she orgasms this way. I know she will.

And she does, throwing her head back with a moaning, stifled scream. She sobs, tears racing down her face at the intensity of what she's feeling.

I rip the tape off her mouth, not wanting to lengthen the torture of that by doing it slow. I reach for my keys and unlock the handcuffs, rubbing her wrists and pulling her front up against mine as she sobs.

Now I get worried I hurt her somehow. "Are you okay? Where did I hurt you?" I ask anxiously, turning her so I can take her face between my hands. I can't believe I hurt her. That was never my intention. I stare into her eyes, searching for that condemnation I'm expecting. A rebuke for the things I did with her.

She shakes her head, sniffling, her eyelashes sticking together from her tears. "You-you didn't." She takes a deep breath. "Hurt me, I mean. It was just." She stops as if to think of what she wants to say next. "It was the most spectacular and. And. I don't know how to say the way I feel. I can't describe it." She leans forward and pecks my lips lightly with hers in the softest, most intimate kiss I've ever had. This moment swells my heart until I feel it might burst. I know it's cliché. My chest can't hold this moment in my heart.

All I can do is hold it close and hope it continues to happen again. And again.

CHAPTER THIRTY-SIX

Conor

I'm sitting in my office watching Savannah. Yes, I admit I'm a stalker. Am I certifiable? Possibly. I not only stalk her, I stalk the men I want to come to their justice.

I watch her when I can, otherwise, I pay people to stalk and follow her and keep her safe. Luckily, I have limitless funds.

It's been three weeks since Dave has attempted getting Savvy into his clutch. Yes, he is the mustache twirling villain in this scenario, and I don't know when he plans to attack again.

I can't keep her under lock and key forever, I can't be like him. I want her to be free and let her out of the cage. Dave wanted to torture her for no reason other than being a sadist, and he could. I want her to live the rest of her life doing what she wants, not what anyone else wants. Whether him or me.

So, she's doing her classes, but I have two people I've hired in each one to make sure she's safe. Following her and friending her. I know, I know. It's a shit thing to do, paying people to befriend her, but I have to have some way to keep her safe when she's not with me. She'll be safe.

Savvy only has two days a week where she has to go to her classes, and today, Friday is the last day this week. She's upstairs in the bathroom finishing getting ready, singing to herself.

The past three weeks have been normal. For us at least. Reel and I are working on looking up our latest victim. Ah hmm. Criminal. He's been out for six years now, and it looks like he's been up to his child porn habits and stalking this whole time. Young girls as young as ten disappear, and we think he's one who is taking them. I can't stalk him during the day, so during the day, Reel and I check on his online habits. He's a fucking waste of human space. Any day now, we will have his daily habits recorded and be able to take him out. No one will miss him. He has no wife or girlfriend. No friends at all. He's the typical degenerate living in the shadows, watching and waiting for his chance to strike.

I hear her footsteps as she hurries down the stairs, running late like usual. It's me. My fault she runs late in the mornings. Sitting back in my chair, I close my eyes and bite my bottom lip, remembering this morning's reason for her lateness.

She woke me by going down on me, my dick in her mouth, deep throating me so far she can't breathe, hands on my balls. I woke up gasping and groaning, my balls emptying down her throat. Best morning wake-up ever. Of course, I had to do the same for her, legs wide, bent and turning out so I have better access to her pussy. Remembering myself balls deep inside her only a half hour ago makes my dick hard as a cement block again. Maybe we have time for another round.

My door is wide open, she runs by it instead of coming in because she knows I'll be ready for another go at the sight of her. I can't get enough. This obsession I have with her is so extreme, to the point I have a hard time concentrating right now. I can't stand her not being in my eyesight.

Another body walks by my door, this time, I scowl, a pulse beats at my temples. It's Will. I keep him around until I can use him. I still don't trust him, but I can use him. Haven't decided how yet.

Savvy walks by again at a more sedate pace, smiling sweetly as she goes by. I don't trust that look. She has something planned, and one I'm sure she knows I won't like.

A few minutes later, with a smirking Riley close behind, her carrying the kitten and Riley carrying all the crap she's bought him. I never knew cats needed all this shit she's gotten him. Carpeted tree, dishes, litter box, toys galore, beds. And I mean beds. The door to his room is now open all the time because he's better. And he has two in our room.

I sit back in my chair, my hands folded across my stomach. "What's going on? What's all this?"

Savvy waves her hand at Riley and grabs a bed with toys out of his hand and places it on the floor, picking up one like a fishing pole with a couple feathers on the end, and waves it at Jason.

She pretends all her attention is on the kitten, twirling the fishing pole for him to jump and chase, I see her eyes jerk to me for a second to see my reaction then back to him.

"Savvy," I say again.

"Yes?" Her voice is so full of fake innocence I would laugh, except Riley is doing it for me. I glare at him, daring him to laugh it up if he wants to live more than a few hours. His mouth straightens out, the ends still twitch as if he can't help himself.

"Why is the kitten in my office?" I say with more patience than I feel. With her, I will force it into my new mental infrastructure. I will rebuild myself for her and only her.

"Well, I'm going to be gone for quite a while today, and you're going to be home, so I thought he could spend the day with you." She continues setting up an area for him in a corner of the room as she talks as if I'm going to agree. I probably will, but I'm going to make her work for it and give me something in return for it. Wink wink.

"Savvy, I'm not going to be able to take care of him for you. I'm working," I argue wanting her to get her back up and argue back. I like it when she shows me backbone.

"But, Conor, he's so easy to take care of. He'll sleep for a few hours after he plays and eats." She bats her eyelids at me a few times and bites her bottom lip. I'm a goner. I slap my hands on the top of the desk, startling both her and Jason, they both jump in the air, the kitten with more agility. He flips around, jumping onto the leg of my desk and clumping up the side until he falls off. I don't want her to know the truth yet. That I'll give her whatever she wants. If she wants the stars, they're hers. The moon, that, too. And if she wants our world, I'll move the galaxy to give it to her.

"Conor. Please."

I wipe my hand down my face, scowling at the object of my displeasure batting at a ringing ball. Fuck my life.

"Okay. You're not going to be able to go to classes today, anyway," I say, ready for the blow-up, and I wait. One. Two.

"What? Of course, I'm going." She tsks at me, shaking her head and smiling like I told her a joke. It's no joke. I was going to tell her that I need him to help me. I talked with Reel and he convinced me I can trust him to help. I need more help with this operation, and Riley will make a good second. I'm going to have him tail Kirk Wilson, find his habits and how he finds the girls. I can't stand the thought, but we'll have to let him take one. My skin crawls at the thought, I don't know how else to stop the whole operation. If I call the cops, they might screw it up again. Fuck. I hate myself if I have to do this.

"No. You're not. There's no choice. I need Riley to do something for me."

"What?" she demands, her fists on her plump hips, body leaning toward me. Her body vibrates with her anger, ready to take off and fly at me.

"Something," I answer vaguely. She doesn't need to know what I do and have done. It's a necessity. That's why I'm damned and the king of my hell. I will take Kirk Wilson down with me, showing what a devil can truly be and what hell is like for the almost living, which he will be when I get a hold of him.

"Something?" she repeats in a high-pitched tone, making fun of my answer to her. "What the fuck kind of answer is that?"

I'm getting tired of this. I'm not used to being questioned, and I've given her a lot of leeway. I've had enough. I slam my hands down on my desk hard enough to make the keyboard of my computer jump. A lot harder than I did before. "Enough."

Her mouth opens, she has no idea what to say. No comeback. Savvy's not scared of me. I can see that, but she's confused. I can see her brain working. Thinking out ways to get around my edict. She must have finally realized she has no choice.

"Fine," she spits the word out. "I'm going outside in the sun and to get away from you, Lord and Master."

"Good. But realize that smart mouth will only get you punishment later. And not one you'll like," I say and watch as she visibly shivers at the idea. She's becoming a slut for my punishments.

She turns and walks out the door, her head held high. I'm not sure why, but that worries me. She agreed too fast. She's up to something. But what?

CHAPTER THIRTY-SEVEN

Savannah

He thinks he has the right to tell me what to do? Fuck that. I'm not going to give up my new life for the imagined diabolical crimes of my husband. It's been three weeks since the thing with Will. Maybe he's given up and finally realizes we're done. I don't know how long it's going to take for this divorce to go through, but it can't be soon enough for me.

I walk out the front door as if I have no plan. And I don't have a plan, I can come up with one. A light breeze ripples through my hair, brushing over my face. The morning sun is slowly warming the late summer morning.

Pulling my upper and lower lips into my mouth, I gaze around the gorgeous grounds. This place is really amazing. But I have to figure out a way to get out. I already have my books in the car Conor bought me. A new Mustang. Red Mustang. He does everything he can for me, and I lo... no, I can't go there. He's so successful and put together, he won't keep me around. An old, used-up housewife like me. He can get any young woman he wants.

I stroll around the front of the mansion, pretending to look at the beautiful roses along one side. I continue on my way to the garage, the doors already open. Keys are already in the front pocket of my jeans, purse in the car next to my book bag.

Opening the door, I get behind the wheel, starting the car. The passenger door opens, and I jerk my head to the side to find Will getting in the seat.

"What are you doing?" I ask. "You're not supposed to leave the house."

He shakes his head. "You can't go by yourself. I know Dave has been quiet the last few weeks, but don't get too comfortable. He's just biding his time. He's unscrupulous. Will do anything to get what he wants. And for some reason, he wants you."

"Gee, thanks for that," I say dryly.

"I don't mean it that way, and you know it," he says, laughing at my response.

Suddenly, a wave of nausea pounds my stomach so hard I have to throw open my door and race back out to the roses and throw up. I've only had coffee, so brown is all that comes up. I heave a couple more times, tears well, and my nose clogs from the force which had overtaken me. A hand appears in my line of sight, holding out a wad of tissues, and another holds my hair back, and I remember the vomit break I had when I got up this morning, and it hits me. I haven't had my period since I got here. I should have had it weeks ago. At least three weeks. We haven't used protection, and I can't remember when I'm due for my shot. I never thought I could get pregnant. Dave always said it was my fault. Of course, it's not like the reason I haven't could be him. I want to cry with happiness, I am finally having a baby, and sad at what Conor might say. I spit a couple of times and wipe my mouth with the tissues. Wish I had water to gargle this vomit taste away.

The hands disappear, and I go to turn away when a small bottle of water is held out to me. I glance up, and Will has a frown of worry on his face. I open the bottle, taking a large gulp into my mouth and spit it out. I do this once more.

"Thank you, Will."

"Are you? I mean should you go to the doctor?" The frown is still there, his hands scrubbing at each other in his stress of not knowing what to do.

I glance around, worried we'll be found out if we stay here much longer. "We've got to get out of here before someone notices."

"Whatever you need, Savvy. I'm so ashamed of what I did for money. Who knows what could have happened if Riley hadn't been there. I will protect you with my life." He thrusts his skinny chest out as if he could protect me from an attacker. A seventeen-year-old kid. I'm not going to embarrass him by saying he can't.

"Thank you. Let's go and see if we can get out of here. I'll stop at the pharmacy on the way to school. You have classes today?" I start my car, glancing around, expecting Conor or Riley to jump in front of the car. Riley is with

Conor and doing stuff for him so much he must be like his right-hand man or something.

I don't look at Will as I drive down the long driveway to the gate. Will slouches in his seat, making himself as small and unnoticeable as possible. The closer I get, sweat beads on my forehead; my mouth goes dry, and a smile clings to my face as if it's fastened unevenly. I know we both look as guilty as shit.

Putting my right foot lightly on the brake to slow us down, my left jumps up and down in time to the intense, wild, uneven beat of my heart rate. I stop at the guard house, not recognizing the man. He must be new.

He bends down to look at me, hoping he hasn't received an order to send me back inside like a prisoner.

"Ma'am."

"Hi, he's feeling sick so we're going to the doctor. Can you open the gate, please?" The last two words I say are said in such a high tone I'm surprised he doesn't realize I'm full of shit.

"Sure, ma'am. Right away." He runs back to the guard house, pressing the button to open the gate. I let out a huge breath, not believing we got away with it. When the gate opens far enough, I switch my foot to the gas, surging through the gate, and make a left with a squeal of burning rubber.

Will sits back up, saying, "I can't believe we did it. He's going to get in so much trouble."

Now, I feel guilty. Thanks for that, Will.

"Let's get to the pharmacy and then to classes." Is all I say. There's nothing else.

It takes twenty minutes to get to the closest one, Conor doesn't live close to the city. His mansion was here before the Bay's built the lake and the city. His great-grandfather wanted his family away from the tainted city of Los Angeles.

Will waits for me in the car; I still don't know what the classes are he's taking. That's not important right now, what is is getting this pregnancy test, going into the bathroom, and taking it. Rip off the Band-Aid as the saying goes.

With the test paid for and stick peed on, I stand at one of the sinks, waiting for the timer to end. One more second, but I don't need it. It shows in two bright pink stripes. Pregnant. I'm pregnant with a man who's not my husband's baby.

I'm in total shock and walk back to my car like a zombie. My mind a complete blank at what I found; even if I already suspected, it's still a shock.

I open the car door and sink into the driver's seat, the leather wraps around my body. I don't even want to go to classes now. I want to be alone and swathe this prospect in cotton, holding it close like the baby is already here.

"So, is it positive?"

When I don't answer and stare into the windshield as if it can tell me what to do, he asks, "It's negative? Tell me."

"It's positive." I have the test wrapped in the brown, rough paper towels from the bathroom to keep and show Conor at some point. Not sure when. "Let's go to classes."

I want to pretend my life is normal for now. I might not be able to concentrate, but I don't want to go back yet. Don't want to think. Only act normal.

CHAPTER THIRTY-EIGHT

Conor

I shouldn't be surprised she snuck out. I should have fired the guard, but it's really not his fault he let her leave, it's the fault of whoever trained him. I smile in pride at her perseverance. She thought it all out and did what she wanted. The tracker in her new Mustang says she's in school, I'll let her stay for now. She has the guards in her classes and Will, although he's probably in his, not with her.

Jason plays with his toys as I sit at my desk, staring into space. I can't get her out of my mind. I'm glad I have Riley looking up Kirk because my interest is only on Savvy. On her ass, her body, her brilliant smile brightening up my day.

Sharp needles of pain climb up my right leg, I start to kick out, and I see it's Jason climbing up my leg, gazing up at my face with intense concentration. He's on his way to my crotch, so I grab him by his scruff, holding him in front of my face. He hangs limp, looking back at me as if studying, trying to decide if I'm nice. I don't know what the fuck he's thinking. He is cute, not quite as white with little patches of red on his ears and body. His fur is getting a little longer.

I set him on my desk, which is a mistake, the pens are great to bat right off the desk. He glances down at one hanging off the edge. He glances at me, an eagerness in his bright eyes. He takes one front foot, and with a little twist, the pen falls off the edge. He follows it with his eyes, his neck and head bow forward, wanting to see where it goes. His body starts to follow, and my hands shoot out, not wanting him to get hurt. Savvy would kill me.

He gives a wide yawn in my hands, and I get up, carrying him to the bed, laying him down. He curls into a little ball and, purring, gets ready for a nap. I can't believe I'm doing this for her. Babysitting a kitten. Fuck, she's got me wrapped around her finger.

I stand back up and walk back to my desk. Sitting back down, I lean forward, staring at the screen which wavers in front of my eyes as I yawn as big as Jason did. Leaning back, my spine cracks. Fuck, I'm tired. I've got to work on this mess with Kirk. I know I've got Riley and Reel on it, I'm sure there's more I can find if I dig harder.

My cell rings, and with my hand over my eyes, I pick it up without looking at the number. "Yeah?" I yawn again. I can't remember the last time I took a nap, but with all this fucking shit going on, I might have to.

"She's been taken." A female voice I don't recognize says.

I'm instantly wide awake. No nap needed now. I stare down at the phone to see who's calling. A number I don't recognize. "Who is this?"

"Sir, sorry, sir. It's Janice, one of the guards with Savannah. We were walking around the back of a building, and I was hit from behind. I was unconscious, sir. They took me to the hospital. I just woke up, and no one here knows about her. She must have been taken. I'm sorry, sir."

I jump up from my chair, yelling, "Riley!"

"Do you have the numbers of the other guards at the school?" My heart clenches knowing Dave got her and sprint out of my office, meeting him outside the front door.

"Yes, sir," The female guard says, I can hear people talking in the background.

"Call them all and give them an update. Tell them to search the school from top to bottom. I don't care if you have to report a bomb, I want every room in that school searched. Got it?"

"Yes, sir."

"How are you?" I know Savvy is my top priority but I have to consider my people as well. Their health and well-being.

There's a slight hesitation as if I surprised her. "Fine, sir. Thank you for asking."

I hang up and head for my Range Rover, Riley following behind. We're both running. "Savvy's been taken. I want you to head over to Dave's and watch the house. If she's not at school, she'll be there." I throw open the door to the car, getting in and staring at him as I strap on the shoulder strap.

"Should I go to the school first and help look?"

"No-wait. Look for Will. Find him. I'll drive you to the school, you get Will, and I'll go to her car and see if there's anything in there to show where she might be." I slam the door closed and start it up, rolling the window down.

"How do you know where her car is?" Riley hurries to the other side and hops in, rolling his window down.

"Got a tracker on it," I explain and grunt. I speed to the gate, expecting it to be open when I get there. If it's not, I'm driving right through. The gates open slowly, and as I squeeze the Rover through, I gaze down at the side of my car, the side barely a half inch from the edge of gate. My eyes skip to the gaze of the guard, his are wide and scared as his drops to the slight distance as do mine. The SUV slides past, and I concentrate on getting back onto the road.

I race down the streets of Bay City, swerving around other cars, making the trip in ten minutes, which normal driving would be at least twenty. I glance at the tracker, maneuvering around the parking lanes until I'm behind her car. I get out and unlock her car with my key. The car is pretty empty except for her small crossbody bag under the driver's seat. I lock it back up and take it over to the Rover, opening the bag up when I get back inside. Cars honk at me as they drive by, I ignore them. They are nothing to me.

There's the usual stuff. Lipstick, powder compact, tissues, and something wrapped in brown paper towels. I throw Riley a surprised look and unwrap it. It has two pink lines. "What?"

"Is that? Is that a pregnancy stick, boss?"

The empty side says negative, the two lines side says positive. She's pregnant? With my baby.

CHAPTER THIRTY-NINE

Savannah

I groan, rolling over onto my side. My stomach groans, and I think I might vomit. My eyes snap open, and I groan louder than my stomach does. My throat feels like sandpaper, and my mouth is filled with cotton balls. I open and close my mouth a couple times, trying to swallow through the dryness.

Looking down at myself, I see I'm still wearing my clothes from school, and I gaze around the room I'm in. Where am I? My stomach decides to leave my body again and I get up, stumbling, my legs don't want to hold me up, and I vomit on the floor. I sit, my legs crossing in front of me, and lean my head down onto my arms on my legs.

I don't know where I am or what happened. Why can't I remember anything? I remember being at school and leaving the classroom with my new friend Janice, and that's all.

I lift my head, there is a door in the corner that might be a bathroom, I'm not sure I'll make it. My legs are so weak. I really need to pee and find something to drink, even if it's sink water.

Holding onto the bed, I slowly stand, my eyesight sifts and swirls, and I close them until the fogginess in my head dissipates. I open my eyes again, striations across my vision less, and I'm able to see a little better. Holding onto the bed, I shuffle my way to the door, which I hope is the bathroom.

I eye the space between the door and the bed, which I'm holding onto, afraid I'll fall again. I decide to take the chance and tottle to the door as fast as I can. My hand scrambles at the knob, needing it open yesterday. Throwing the door open, not caring it hits the wall with a bang. I run to the toilet, throwing the lid up and vomiting. I'm throwing up so much my stomach feels like it's going to come out my throat, and the pain is intense. Tears well in my eyes, but I don't have the strength to cry. Saliva keeps filling my mouth, and the instant it hits my stomach, I throw that up. I think I might choke on nothing. I can't stop the surging in my stomach.

Lying on the floor, my body jerks with involuntary spasms. I feel like I'm dying, and I want to cry for my unborn baby. I have no more tears left. I curl into a ball, my body still jerking, my mouth opening and throat closing so I can't breathe.

I can hear the door to the bedroom open and footsteps head to where I'm lying. Two sets of steps, I think. I really don't care right now. I hope they kill me and put me out of my misery. And I'm beyond miserable.

"Look at her. You gave her too much ketamine." It sounds like Dave's voice yelling at someone. I don't understand any of this. My body jerks again, and the spasming in my stomach makes my throat close, and I can't breathe.

"Get the doctor. She can't die on me. I need her," he tells whomever he's talking to. I lift my head slightly and drop it immediately to the floor with a faint groan. More of a whimper.

Dave lifts my upper body with one arm and gets his other arm under my legs and lifts me from the floor. He lays me on the bed and covers me with the sheet and comforter. He brings a trash can over just in case. I'm so hot, I try to throw the covers off, but I'm too weak. A second later, I'm freezing and try to burrow further under the covers. It's a vicious, endless cycle. Hot. Cold. Hot. Cold. On and on.

I hear the door open and murmuring voices. I'm too out of it now to pay attention. I'm in a stupor by this time.

Noises come in and out of my hearing. A sharp prick to my arm, which I can't even acknowledge, I'm so oblivious to everything. I black out.

My eyes are closed, and I lie there trying to assess how my body is feeling. I don't know where I am or remember what has happened. I throw my eyes open and stare at a white ceiling. I blink a couple times and turn my head to the left to see an IV stand with a line leading to my hand. The bag is almost empty. I turn my head to the right and find a regular bedroom. It looks like the one I had at Dave's. My heart freezes at the thought. No. It can't be. I can't be back.

My heart restarts, and pain fills my chest at the concept. I raise myself onto my elbows and slowly sit up. I'm so weak. I have to leave; I can't stay, even if I have to crawl out. I throw the covers off and see I'm only wearing a light nightgown. I don't want to know who dressed me in this.

I move my legs off the bed and try to stand on my bare feet. I feel pretty strong and think I can make my way. I take a step and groan. My legs hurt. I slide the needle out of my skin, pressing a finger to the tiny hole to stop any bleeding, the pain in my legs urging me on. I shuffle my feet, making my way carefully to the door.

Pressing my ear to the door, I listen and only hear silence. No footsteps, no voices, no nothing. I reach out, taking the doorknob in my hand, and turn it. Slowly and carefully. It gives a light click, and I wait to see if someone hears and comes.

Nothing. I open the door only wide enough to fit my face through. My eyes shoot from side to side, seeing no one in the hallway. Where is everyone? It can't be this easy. It can't.

I open the door wider, wide enough for my body to fit through. I put a hand on my belly where my baby lies. I don't want him or her being born in this hell hole. I will do everything I possibly can to make that not happen.

Creeping down the hallway, I walk on my toes and balls of my bare feet so they don't make any noise. I reach the stairs at the end of the hall, looking over the banister and the corner, not being able to see anyone from this angle.

This is just way too easy. I know it's a trick, but I have to do this anyway, even if it is. The stairs and downstairs are carpeted, so no one will hear me.

I take one step at a time, stopping to listen after each step-down. I go to take the last step-down, and a voice makes me slump my shoulders.

"Well, well, well. Look who's feeling better. Come to beg your husband to forgive you and take you back?"

I turn my head and see Dave standing by the entrance to the kitchen. "How did I get here?"

"Well, *wife.*" He emphasizes the word. "I paid someone to bring you back. They just used too much force." He frowns at the memory. "I can't use you dead."

I straighten my back, not allowing him to browbeat me like he always used to. Conor taught me one thing. How to stand up for myself. My brain races as I try to think of what to do. I know Conor is looking for me. He wouldn't abandon me. Would he? I know he wouldn't.

"I'm not your wife anymore. We are separated. Release me."

He bursts out laughing as if I said the best joke he ever heard. "No." That's it. No.

"You can't keep me here," I say shrilly, starting to panic, resting one hand on my belly.

Dave sees the gesture; his eyes shoot back up to mine. "So, you're pregnant already?"

"No." I spit out, throwing my hand away. "I still feel sick."

"I'll have the doctor come back to check on you. Maybe you need more fluids from the sedative." He strolls over to me, hands in the front pockets of his slacks.

"I'm fine now."

"I also want him to take your blood for a pregnancy test. Can't raise some other man's bastard child. I'll have you given an abortion."

"No. Never." I step back, and he rushes me, grabbing me by the back of my neck, tilting my head back to look up at him. Fear clogs my brain, and for a minute, I can't think. I can only tremble in his hands.

"Hummm." He leans his head closer, running his nose along the side of my face as he breathes deeply. "Maybe I can use this."

"I won't let you kill my baby. All the years we were married, and you never gave me one. Must be a reason. Right?" He snarls at my words, and I know I hate him. If this were any other man, I wouldn't care. We'd be in this together, but he always blamed me for not getting pregnant, and it was never my fault.

Dave shakes me like a dog shakes a toy, I don't care as long as he doesn't hurt my baby. He still holds me close to him by the back of my neck. "I will force you to have an abortion if you try to leave me. A senator needs a wife by his side, and you are it, and if you're pregnant, that's a plus."

I try to shake my head no, but he interrupts.

"Also, if you don't, I'll have him put in prison for vigilantism. He's put so many, many men there, he won't last long. So, that's your choice. You and your baby or his life." He tosses me away, and I stumble, my hands on the wood banister holding me up. Choice. That's not a choice.

CHAPTER FORTY

Conor

Both Riley and I sit in the Mustang, watching the house. We've been here all night, and I'm not about to leave until I have her. I sent for the Range Rover, which someone had picked up from the university and brought back home. Now it's coming here so Riley and I can switch off for getting food and bathroom breaks. Unfortunately, nature has to come first.

This is taking too long. My instincts say run in and take him and anyone else there down. He could be hurting her. Has she told him about the baby?

I pound my fists against the steering wheel, we hear a crack. It can't stand the fury filling me, wanting release. I'm a volcano waiting to erupt. And God help anyone in its way.

"Boss, we'll get her. She's strong. Smart. She'll figure something out." Riley nods a couple of times as if to emphasize himself.

My heart starts pounding so hard and unevenly, the feeling goes up my throat, and I feel like I'm having a heart attack. I gasp from the sharp, stabbing pain of the squeezing of the organ. Hope not. I can't help her if I'm in the hospital or dead.

My phone rings, and I glance down, seeing it's Reel. I have to get a hold of myself, I send the call to the car.

"Reel."

"I haven't gotten much yet. He's good, but we already knew that by the way he's been able to cover his tracks all these years. I was able to track a call to a doctor from his phone yesterday. A Doctor Harrelsen. That's it so far. As soon as I get more, I'll let you know. Dave might have another phone he's gotten. I'm searching for that."

"Thanks, man. I have people going through cameras and asking anyone if they saw anything," I say, running my hand over the top of my head and lowering it until my forehead rests on the steering wheel. I'm bone tired, and I know mistakes can happen, I have no choice. I won't let anything else happen to her. I can understand why she did the things she did, I just wish she hadn't. This wouldn't have happened. I can't even blame Will, he was following Savvy's lead and trying to help her in his young mind. He is only seventeen, I've learned.

There's a honk behind us, and I glance in the rearview mirror, my Range Rover. I'm going to kill whoever drove it and honked. This might give Dave an advantage over us if he or one of the neighbors heard and calls the police.

I open the door and get out, gazing around to see if anyone else saw or heard anything. Riley is doing the same. The man who drove the SUV here gets out himself, walking over as if he carried out an important errand. He did, he only finished it wrong.

He's young, I'll give him that, but he might have jeopardized Savvy by the honk.

"Hey..."

That's all he's given to say. "You're fired."

"But..."

I grab him by the front of his shirt and yank him close. Close enough I don't have to shout. Even this might attract unwanted attention. I make my words as heavy and dark as I can, wanting to put as much fear into him as I can. "That honk might have ruined everything. This is an undercover mission. We are trying to *not* be noticed."

"I'm sorry. I'll do better. This is my first time." His young, earnest face makes guilt drip through me. Savvy is changing me from the hard, unfeeling man I have to be to someone with feelings. Someone with feelings to want to give him another chance. That's not who I need to be for her, the baby, our way of life. Cutthroat. That's who I am. I can't start second guessing who is going to pay. If they have a wife. A girlfriend. Children. What they have done never bothered them with other's families. Why should I care about theirs?

I yank him even closer, pissed I'm going to do it. "If you ever fucking do something like that without thinking of the consequences, I *will kill you*. Understand?" I don't think I can make myself any clearer. His eyes go big, his pale face gets even paler.

"Y-yes, s-ir," he stutters the words, his voice as scared as his face.

I push him away so hard he stumbles back against the Rover, thudding as he falls, and I glare at him making a noise, even though it was my fault.

He gazes around, I'm sure wondering how he's going to get back to the mansion. No buses come to this area. I raise my eyebrows, waiting for his comment. Instead, he stumbles away, pulling his phone out of his pocket.

"Harsh," Riley says beside me, a smile in his tone.

The only sound around us is the soft wind brushing the leaves through the trees. The street traffic is far enough away you can barely hear it from here, this isn't a gated community, but there's still not much traffic. A few workers trucks, that's it.

"I'm going to get us something to eat. Be back soon. Anything in particular you want?" he asks as I toss him my set of keys. The kid, I don't even know his name, still has the other set. He better give those back.

"Nothing for me." I shake my head. I'm not hungry at all, in fact, I'm afraid if I eat, I might chuck it back up.

"I'll get you some pancakes and coffee. That might help. You gotta eat and drink something. You'll dehydrate, otherwise. What good will you be to her if you get weak." He lays his hand on my forearm for a minute, leaving me alone to get back in the red Mustang I'm sure won't cause any attention.

I shove two fingers into my closed eyelids, rubbing them. Opening them back up, I tilt my head way back, the cracking sound a relief. I tilt my head to the house, watching nothing. Nothing is happening. I can't do nothing any longer. I'm not a wait-and-see kind of guy. I'm an action guy, and this sitting and doing nothing is killing me slowly.

That's it. I can't wait any longer. I open the car door, slamming it closed, not caring if anyone fucking hears.

Across the street, I run to the house, my boots clomp so loud I'm surprised the whole block can't hear as I race across the street. I can't pay attention to how beautiful it is or a quarter the size mansion mine is. I pound up the walkway leading up to the front door, pounding my fist on it. We're going to have it out now. I *will* get them back.

My hands in fists as I open and close them impatiently, my body feels enclosed in concrete, and I will detonate, exploding the fragments of Dave's life into millions of pieces in the wake of my eruption.

The door finally opens to Dave, leaning a forearm against the frame of the door, voice excited, face calm and serene. He greets me as if we're still friends. "Hey, buddy. Haven't seen you in a while. What do you want?"

"You know what I want," I grit through clenching teeth.

"My wife? Sorry, no. She's staying with me. We're back together now." His smile switches to a look that is as malicious as it can get. He's enjoying himself too much and has something up his sleeve waiting to reveal it to me. He's so full of himself. He thinks he holds all the cards, and I'm the lone joker in the deck.

"I want to see her."

"No, I'm sorry. It's not possible right now. She's lying down. Doctor's orders." He smiles and smirks, knowing he holds all the cards and all the kings and queens, even the ace.

"I'm not leaving until I see her. I want her to tell me she wants to stay." I can't stand the look of triumph exploding over his face.

"Well, let me see how she's feeling in her delicate condition." He closes the door, making me stand outside and wait.

That lets me know he knows she's pregnant. Why will he want her to stay there with another man's baby inside her? This isn't making any sense to me. I don't know what ace he has, but it worries me. He's too confident.

The door opens again, and Savvy leans against the frame as if it's holding her up. She's way too pale. I reach out to grab her, but she jerks away so I can't touch her.

"Savannah, why are you here? Let me take you back home." I hold my hand out to her, wishing and hoping she'll take it. Instead, she holds her hand in a fist close to her abdomen as if forcing herself from taking mine.

"No, Conor. I've decided I was wrong to leave my husband. My place is beside him as he runs for the senate. I shouldn't have left in the first place. Thank you for giving me the space to learn my own feelings."

She sounds like she's reciting something written out for her. Her voice is frozen and wooden. This isn't her, but there is nothing I can do about it. I see something in her eyes. Fear. Something dark. There's also a new strength

I've seen growing in her. Pride for her wells but also a deep sadness that in her new growth, I might lose her. I can't. I won't. I'll do everything I can to bring her back.

I want to scream and yell my objections. Ask why she's doing this, but I know why. She's protecting me. I don't know what Dave has on me, I'll have to have Reel look into it.

The metallic taste of blood fills my mouth, and I realize I've bitten the inside of my lip so hard I bit through.

My heart pounds so hard the blood pulses through my veins like a herd of wild horses. For the first time in. Forever. Tears burn in my eyes; I think I might lose it if I stand here much longer. I don't remember the last time I cried. Maybe when my parents and sister died in the car accident? I don't think I did when my wife died, I think I was emotionally dead by then. I won't let him see how affected I am. He can't have that satisfaction.

This is her decision, even if I want to capture her and drag her out. I can't do that.

Even though I know her words aren't how she feels, they still sink into my gut like a leaden weight, a cold knife stabbing over and over into my heart.

Dave's wife and my baby will have to stay here.

For now. I will get them back and end his reign of terror for her. I *will* find out his secrets. I know they are deep, dark, and depraved. All of them, and then I will end him.

THE END

FOR NOW

LOOK FOR DELICIOUS VENGEANCE COMING SOON

SAVANNAH

I'm back with my husband, Dave Collier. He's threatened my baby, Conor's baby, and says he has proof to put Conor in prison. So, here I am playing the dutiful wife. But I'm slowly dying inside.

I was free for one month, and I'm dying for that freedom. I had one brief glimpse, and it was snatched away.

I'm losing myself in what Dave wants, and I'm afraid he'll get all of me. Even my life.

About the author

I'm a dog groomer by day and a writer by night. I live in Southern California with my cats. Yes I am the old woman with all the cats you hear about.

Feel free to follow me in all my locations!

https://linktr.ee/dastein

Also by

BRUTAL SAVIOR

Merciless Few MC

Hidden Hills, Illinois

NOW IN KINDLE UNLIMITED

It's love at first sight for Slayer.

When I first lay eyes on Molly Marino, I'm captivated by her innocent beauty, even as she strips at the club Sinsations. My heart leaps, my stomach drops, and I'm struck dumb.

Seeing those men salivating over her makes me want to kill every last one of them, or at least stab them in the eyes with a rusty fork. But then, I learn she's the sole supporter of her one-year-old daughter, and it terrifies me. I don't know anything about kids. I'm a bad man who's done many bad things for the Merciless Few Motorcycle Club. But Molly and her daughter might be my only chance at redemption.

When they are kidnapped, a war ignites, bringing different factions together to save them. I will unleash my club and the fires of hell to protect them.

MOLLY

My brother-in-law has kidnapped me, planning to use and abuse me like a toy with his friends. I'm falling into a deep, dark well of despair. But I can't give up. I have to find a way to claw my way out for my daughter.

Thinking of her is the only thing keeping me from surrendering. I'll do whatever it takes to keep her safe.

STEP DIAMOND

IN KINDLE UNLIMITED

I'm late to my stepfather's baseball game.

We haven't seen each other since I left for university and my mother died. Now I'm off for summer break and he's even more sexy now than ever.

A woman is getting her claws into him, her slimy insidious whispers of how they can be together winning him over.

He fights me and what we can be at every suggestion and attempt to bring us closer. I know he wants me but he fights us. Fights me. Denies what we can be. He's my daddy, he won't admit to it. Yet.

But that woman who wants him, who thinks he's hers. She has another thing coming. Me.

Will she win or will I kick her to the curb?

SECOND CHANCE LOVE

In kindle unlimited

Angelina Van Halen

I'm in Sin City the day before Valentine's to go to the Bay Brothers rock concert with my son and his fiance'. This might be the band's last one and my heart beats for only one. Rhett Bay and I were once a thing before my father decided I had to marry for the family. That's what the mafia does. Right? So, I did. Now forty years later I'm seeing him in concert and I want him again. What happens in Vegas, stays in Vegas.

Rhett Bay

This might be our last concert. My brothers haven't decided yet and I'll go along with whatever they decide. I've never been married and even though I'm in my sixties I'm still having the time of my life. A new girl every day. Who cares if they're young enough to be my daughter. And my grandnephew reminded me. Young enough to be my granddaughter. F###. I need to find someone my own age. Then I find Angelina again.

CRUEL INTERCEPTION

Nicole

I've always been attracted to my best friend's boyfriend who's a star defensive tackle for the Bay City Panthers football team. He was never interested in me. Ruby and football was all he ever cared about. They've broken up now and now's my chance and I'm going to take it.

Justin

I've never been interested in my ex's friend but now

I'm seeing her in a new light. She's gorgeous in an exotic sexy I-don't-know-I-am way. But how do I get by her brother's, especially Leo who's in charge of of the Italian/American mafia here in Los Angeles.

HIS CHRISTMAS GIFT

Griffin

I take what I want. I've fought to get where I am and I'm at the top. My partner has embezzled millions of dollars and I know what I want in return. His daughter.

Katrina

I've always been in love with Griffin Van Halen, even as a little girl. I'm now an intern at his and my father's publishing company and find out he's embezzled millions. In return Griffin wants me for three months. To keep my father out of prison I have to do it. Being Griffin's plaything can't be that bad. Right?

Not your usual Christmas romance.

Trigger: mentions rape

STEP PUCK

I'm the number one goalie for the Bay City Brawlers Hockey Team. We only have one more game until the Stanley Cup and it's ours. We have to win because this will be my last game. At thirty-five I'm done. Done with the bullshit fights. Done with the pain that will now be with me for the rest of my life. And that's what I finally want. A life.

She walks back into my life uninvited. The little step-sister I haven't seen in five years. Sexy, unattainable twenty-one years old and not for me. Except she still follows me around and there's a connection I can't ignore.

I've always been in love with Billy Wallace. Ever since his dad married my mom when I was four. Now I'm twenty-one and know what I want. And I'm going to get him and he can't ignore me. He can't ignore our connection and I won't fail.

TRIPLE PUCK PLAYERS

I'm in lust with three players of the Bay City Brawlers Hockey Team. The Triple Threat they are called, Jesse Barone, Hutch Adams and Abel Wayne. I'm tired of dating the men my father, country singer Brett Perkins suggests. Suggests. Pushes.

I'm finally going to meet them at the championship after party.

Jesse is the protector of the bunch. Hutch, the caring fun-loving goof. Abel, the financial genius as well as a genius on the ice.

Their brawling tendencies gets them into trouble all the time. They bowl through the opposing team, leaving havoc and destruction.

TRIPLE PUCK VALENTINES

Our team of four is broken.

Or is it?

In the middle of the hockey season I have to go back to Texas on a family emergency. I planned on going alone, but Kat insists on going with. I can't convince her to stay in Bay City. I will protect her at all cost.

For the first time our Triple Threat of the Bay City Brawlers will be separated. Abel and Jesse will have to work double duty.

But the Triple Threat will protect her from the threat that has haunted me my whole life and kept me away from my family. Protect everyone from a devastating secret.

A threat of hatred for anyone that doesn't feel the same way they do. We will stop them. No matter the cost.

Printed in Dunstable, United Kingdom